BARKING UP THE WRONG GEEK

By Lauren Wolpert

ISBN 978-0-578-90686-7

Published by Waltzing Gorillas
www.waltzinggorillas.com

Printed in the United States of America

To Sydni,
Who I love . . .
Who taught me to celebrate.

"You're only given a little spark of madness.
If you lose that, you're nothing."

Robin Williams

ACKNOWLEDGEMENTS

Brenda Littleton and Harvest Project with help to manifest this and other projects to completion.

Melanie Pahlmann and Bill Georgevich at Lucid Design Studios for their editorial, design and publishing expertise.

Susan Rukeyser and Desert Split Open for reading and workshopping place.

Deborah Tobin and Beatnik Lounge, continued support and creative outlet.

Lolly Goodwoman and Stagefright. Because who else will let me play the keyboard with a dildo while wearing a onesie.

INTRODUCTION

No chickens were injured in the writing of *Barking Up the Wrong Geek*. It is a work of fiction. No character is based on a real person.

Alcohol is not a potato; alcohol is the end result of a breaking down, a fermentation process of change. This story is a ride, not a read: your kinesthetic feel of the story is more important than any plot or character.

Give up all illusions of what is called real and fall into the one law of cause and effect.

The emotions are real and true. Whichever younger me wrote this, I'd like to thank them for their diligence in withstanding the endeavors that contribute to the present me. In other words, I want to thank the early me for pulling down my pants, rather than giving me a wedgie.

Sure it's dark. The dark is where the meek can be.

The meek aren't going to inherit the earth, so we've taken the night.

A BEGINNING

Considering the mess that must have been left after the suicide, Bart felt they did a fairly good job of cleaning this reasonable-rate one bedroom, one bath, plus sofa bed, no cooking or entertaining-allowed room. Though the wallpaper was darker in some places, the bathroom was very clean. That was important for a man with two children in his keep.

If he hadn't heard the stories about the late-night ambulance or felt the whispers in the motel walls, Bart might have thought the darkened wallpaper was left long ago by the fellow who had lost his hardware store or by the young solider with neither wife nor legs. Bart looked at the rug and wondered how to phrase his questions on the removal of blood stains without raising uncalled-for attention on why that would be important to him or how he would know that there was blood spilled to begin with.

The proprietor thought he had pulled a fast one over on Bart. Bart let him; took the room and the rate. Still, Bart would have liked to have asked about the stain remover. Bart had his own reasons for respecting a good stain remover, above and beyond a good stain. He would break into the house keeper's closet and check the buckets for his answer. He would also take a towel or two. That was going to be his pay for losing. That seemed a reasonable rate for Bart's failure.

It was hard to believe that no one else had found this note. There must have been so many other things to do—call the police, tag the body. There might have been an autopsy. That would be a waste of time and money. Maybe even a guilt-ridden relative hoping for a mattress full of cash and a safety deposit key. There were tears shed. There was no key. The mattress was just a stop for slumber and struggle. Beyond that, a vacant room to let.

Bart inspected the envelope. Bart thought, "bang bang," as his hairy knuckles tore open the seal.

As he read the note, Bart wondered who would find it interesting. Or why would someone without hope think anyone would care at all about anything they had to say? Why would someone who didn't care anymore think anyone else would care? Why would he care if he didn't care? Writing a suicide note should negate the need for the suicide. He could have just written, "I am not loved; I have no money." or "I have no money; I am not loved. Instead, he droned on and on about the murder and how he loved her, and he couldn't live without her, and she certainly couldn't live with him because she was now dead. When he put the gun to his head, mouth, throat, he must have looked like a sad cat who just ate his best friend.

If Bart was ever entrusted to give a young man advice, it would be to write your suicide note in your teen years. Give it the vibrant rage of a young man.

Then when the time comes to take your own life, you are not left with a drooling mulling dower note. We can all do better than that. Bart resisted the urge to correct since there was no one left to shame.

Bart was a man who knew a thing or two about humans and all who identified themselves as such. He wondered what he could have gotten from the dead man if he had lived. If that were the case, where would he have stayed this night at a rate so cheap? There was no one to thank. Bart doubted he would.

Bart didn't like people, in the *per se* humanist form of them. He liked their problems. Not in the way of someone who says, "I'm a good listener" and gets their self-worth from sitting and nodding, like a bobble head. It was like, "I'm good with animals," meaning, "I haven't been bitten recently. Last time I lost a finger. Not the important one." He considered people's problems pennies that he would one day take into Coinstar for something that weighed less than a pound.

Bart found the envelope containing the suicide note when he swung one side of the bureau away from the wall. He planned to tape his cash reserve into an out-of-the-way spot, close to the mirror. If the urge to spend came over him, he could look into his beady eyes and ask himself, nose to nose, the question, "Do I want to spend this money? *Can* I spend this money?" Bart was not a gullible man, but he was a good liar. He believed everything he said to himself. He spent his money.

Bart felt behind the bureau spot. A much better, safer

place than between the box spring and mattress or under the rug. Since traveling he'd been hit in both places, fortunately during days of smaller fortune.

The note must have been flung behind the dresser in a fit of blood and regret. It was the second note he had found in his lifetime. Bart blew into the envelope and made the wish that he was on the receiving end of some monetary good fortune. He was.

He cast aside the final words when he saw that the envelope held a five-dollar bill. Bart was puzzled by the cash. Was this the total of the man's estate? Bart was guessing his gender, considering suicide to be a man's game: Woman's league: cutting and puking.

Had the recently deceased lived in this room for a multitude of days, or was he an especially good tipper compared to the rest of the masses who changed beds faster than an accelerated game of duck, duck, goose?

Only the good die young: the solider, the saint, the tipper. Then again, Bart thought the body could have been one of those college boys who bring their last breaths and regrets to the doorsteps of the alien class they think of as romantic. The men who have P.O. boxes on streets called Main and Broadway and have never pulled their father's Lexus into a circular driveway off of lanes called Petunia or Spruce.

The honest, hardworking washerwoman who tended to this man's linens and towels in his last days of desolation and a few exhausted tears would never accept the five dollars blood money. Bart slipped the bill into his wallet and vowed to live forever. He wrote on the envelope: Cocoa Puff, Kool Aid, bologna, bread, coffee, chicken.

Lester and Lestim sat back-to-back in the corner of the room where they could catch a few last rays of the sun before it sunk behind a neighboring brick wall—the last few rays that made the dust dance and their eyes turn sleepy. They sat back-to-back, that being the only way they can sit, considering they are siblings who share a rectum. They sucked on opposite ends of the worn but friendly towel. Bart was glad they hadn't suckled the soap before his shower. It wasn't that he didn't love them, because he didn't, or that they disgusted him, for they did, or that what they had was contagious, which it wasn't. He made his living from their ability to entertain by biting the heads off live chickens, and since two are better than one, two connected as they were, it really kept the greenbacks turning over. Bart liked his job as much as he could stand the disappointment of his life.

Bart could never bring himself to use a piece of soap after they had violated it, especially as they got older. It was something he could ignore when they were four or five, but now that they were hovering over twelve, he couldn't bring himself to bathe with any object incased in their saliva and he would never spend the money on something like soap, towels or shoe-shining strips that within the natural order of the traveling man were theirs for the taking. He wondered if the envelope had a third side for his "things to do."

The children playing quietly in the corner, the erratic suicide note, the long drive; the five dollars created a haze of reminiscence of summer days, fishing in the lake and the seeing of the first dead body he ever saw. It wasn't red and gruesome, protruding from the windshield of a car bought with earnings from a part-time job, but blue and bloated, like a Thanksgiving Day float made by three volunteers with a stack of newspapers and left-over paint freed from the edge of the can before it withered and dried.

He and Chuck had been out fishing when they saw an empty rowboat.

Being two healthy-minded young boys, they decided it would be much better to sit in a boat and be bitten by gnats than to sit on the shore and be bitten by gnats. Where better to read *Beaver Digest* and contemplate their own emerging pubic hairs? They found the man with a plaid shirt and live bait, which had multiplied and prospered into a dynasty of sorts. Chuck thought that if they stuck his filet knife into the bloated man, he wouldn't look so ugly. Alas, the poor man didn't debloat, unbloat, inbloat. He bled. In honor of the fellow, let it be remembered that he bled well. Better than better men had bled before him.

The boys left when they realized what smelled, and that the smell was not pretty, not pretty like the bloat-man. They snuck into the back door of the theatre to see a movie they shouldn't see, considering the redundancy of X in the rating. There were no gnats, a couple of spiders, a few maggots, and a flotilla of daddy long legs, plus the cool dampening of pungent summer sweet sweat. Their feet stuck to the floor.

Lester found the soap. That was too bad. At least they were quiet. Bart didn't have to worry if he should feed them now or wait till the show. If they could hold out, their hunger would bring the house down. Let them have the soap. Bart looked forward to finding company for the five-dollar bill that now sat in his wallet without an equal.

Lester is the girl of the twins; Lestim, the boy. Bart had learned that from another note he found. The one pinned to them some seven years before. What he wrote on the back of the paper he had long forgotten. It probably went something like: loaf of bread, quart of milk, dozen eggs. Bart thought back with no regrets. His lists were getting more concise, having lost the "of's," and, like life, more colorful, with at least one and two its colors: the blood red of the children's faces as the decapitated chickens squirted around their mouths, giving them clown lips, and mud brown as it dripped from their chinny, chin chins and on to the tent's dirt floor where, night after night, Bart stood outside his tent and barked for the crowd. "Ladies and Gentlemen, only those of strong faith dare enter here. We are all made in God's image. Even Lester and Lestim? That is the question I ask you tonight. I know them as children. They cry when they are sad. Laugh when they are happy. Where is your compassion, my good people of <u>fill in the</u>

blank?" (Bart never quite cared where he was.) "Will you let these little children come on to you? Or turn your head from these descendants of Adam?"

Bart again looked into the mirror at his own image of God and pulled out a vagrant eyebrow that grew defiantly from the center of his face. He pulled twice on the course hair before it came free. It brought his eyes to water. A weaker man would say a tear.

YOUNG BART

The boys who want to be firemen. Boys who want adventure. Boys who want to farm the land; the ones who want to be like Dad. Told anyone can grow up to be President of the United States of America ... presidents don't wear uniforms and they're not the hero of any childhood games. That's for girls.

His old man eats dirt. Sister picks her nose. He looks up to the sky and falls down on his knees, prays it isn't so, and it rains and is ... so. Mother puts out her cigarette before she starts to cook. Her long wavy girl-like hair stays tied back. A reason to be grateful. He would have a reasonable shot to make it to Congress, but still no hat, no uniform, no hero.

When Bart was a child, adults would pat him on the head and laugh among themselves before granting the moments needed for him to skip away. Bart made note of their ridicule but hid his contempt under peach-fuzzed skin and parted hair. He would sit by a tree stump and reinvent the concept of revenge, only to become pissed when he would discover vengeance has been around longer then fire and has exerted a much greater influence over the creation of civilization then civilization itself. No insult to fire intended.

Bart would check his aging by running a hand across

his face. He would feel for the progress contained within his sideburns. Feel for growth. He once saw a photo taken in Manhattan of Hasidim with black coats, pallid skin, wire-rimmed frames. What he noticed were the locks of hair growing down the side of their faces. That was a source of envy that blossomed into a goal. When he grew up, he promised himself, he wanted to be exactly like them, till someone told him they were Jews. He decided to emulate Elvis instead.

Bart's youth drooled by with a good deal of personal success. He was appreciated by all in his tiny arena: junior high election, most popular fellow, most likely to succeed. Yet when he heard the term "missing link" he found the word needed to express his scorn to those who gazed upon him. As his baby fat fell by the wayside, his bitterness grew, transforming the supple clay of an innocent into the hard body of a young man.

Life should be as sweet as it should be, would be. Bart knew that was his birthright, even if it wasn't right at birth that his rights had begun. There were places for the kind of man Bart was to become. Where one could take an iota of power and explode it to a maximum of gain. For now, student council must do.

Bart Barker, with his small-town brilliance and pizzazz. He was Bart Barker, destiny. The same adults who patted him on his head now slapped him on his back and called him a man, though he heard silence that felt like laughter when his back was turned. A sweep of high achievements held him aloof in the seventh grade. They will lower their eyes when I pass so they will not be blind. Their laughter will cease.

High school plays? Deafened by the silence, the applause was exclusively his. He spat between curtain calls. The redundancy of success felt like failure. He cursed to the mirror as the summer months crawled into Fall. Why should his eyebrows grow together? Could he ever be loved without fear? Could he be trusted? Late into the night, other boys would keep their own company under the cover of the darkness and a greying sheet. Bart would tweeze.

Retiring to the bench during practice, after another touchdown thrown, he dreamed of who should be honored as his homecoming queen. It would not be Nancy. She who, late in August, anticipating the return of Fall, start of school, with nothing to talk about but fading tans and stupid parents, had lain with Bart in the gully between the high school cafeteria and Mr. Parker's house. Bart had taken all the whispered stories he had heard on the porch in front of the post office and was acting them out for his audience and costar Nancy. She pulled his bucking head close to her and whispered, "Elvis, Elvis." He took the disappointment that hung between his legs home, shaved his sideburns to above his ears. No, it would not be Nancy. By October, high school was sideburnless. The only name that would ever be whispered to him again would be Bart.

The coach walked onto the field with a lilt in his step,

it could have been called a happy walk if there was context to understand that concept. There was a young man not even a half pace behind him. The coach said these words Bart hardly heard but would reverberate through his life forever.

"I'd like to introduce you to a new student, Robert Richmond. I'm sure you'll all make him feel right at home." Bart didn't notice his bright blues, full of honesty and strength, or his white-blond hair which waved over his forehead and curled up the nape of his neck as if commanded by a prince in some medieval story book. That was for the girls to notice. The same girls who noticed every zit, pore, and stubble of Bart.

Nancy granting audience in the locker room. Whispered reverb to thundering echoing filled the air with Bart. The only thing for his brain to do was run from his nose and flow from his eyes till he resembled the shine of a freshly baked glazed donut, dropped in the parking lot and brushed off for consumption. The girls soaked up every word and letter that Nancy had to say. When it was time for them to slip into sleep, they would retell the tales to a campfire surrounded by themselves. They would listen and nod and recognize the heroine as a woman they had yet to meet.

Bart wouldn't notice Robert's wide shoulders and firm buttocks, ripe for slapping on the field. Those observations had to be left to the coach. What Bart saw in front of him was a firm, fine set of crescent-shaped brows. All the hair growing in the same direction. Bart feared he looked like a convict. If Bart could be President, Robert could be a man. If Bart could be a man, Robert could be a God.

The concept of trying harder, the spirit of competition, left a bad taste in Bart's mouth. Robert was only a temporary distraction. It was only a matter of time. This was Bart's town.

BART

"Come on down for breakfast, lazy bones." Betty turned from the bacon to slap Barry's hand. He'd already had his bowl of cereal, two English muffins, a short stack, two fired once-over and a couple of links. Betty worried there would be nothing left for her younger, sleepy son Ben. Barry's arteries didn't care.

Bart Barker—husband, father, mayor—was outside. Bart liked to pace around his yard with his coffee in hand. Get some fresh air. Avoid the morning battle the boys always seemed to have. He could deal with the dinner ruckus if only for the practical reason that eating meatloaf, mashed potatoes, and French-cut string beans while prancing around the property promoted the "What's going on in the Barker house?" whispers.

In the morning, with his "World's Greatest Dad" mug that Betty gave him eight years before, signing Barry's name—a cute thing to do, considering Barry was only post-fetal and preoccupied with focusing and unclenching his fists—dealing with the boys' bickering was a problem. At the least it was unpleasant and, besides, Bart had a different agenda.

He dug the toe of his shoe into the mulch around the rhododendron. Chuck wasn't ever much as a fisherman, but now he seemed to have a gift for making things grow.

Chuck learned from his life of shit. Manure was his secret weapon.

Bart acknowledged or ignored his neighbors driving to their jobs, into the city for work. He liked their envy of his extra hour at home with his coffee mug and shrubbery. He pulled a weed and waved the dirt off his hand, being careful of his suit and his shit. His job as mayor was convenient, but after fertilizer and dental bills, it didn't leave much for dry cleaning.

He looked to the back of the yard. There was the old fenced-in dog run right in front of the empty lot where the trees thicken to an area of forest that separated Bart's town from the rest of the world. Ben had been a year old when Bozer died. Here was where he lived and where, in time, he was interred. It was cancer. Betty cried when they finally put him down, but the poor thing was in pain. It would have been cruel to let him live.

Bart figured that after six years in the grave, there would be nothing left but bones for another dog that he promised to get the boys.

Bart thought he heard children's laughter coming from the woods. His kids were safe inside. Assuming a family is a safe place for children. Chuck's two girls? He couldn't remember them ever laughing.

Distracted by the sound of the diesel engine of a new Mercedes turning over down the street, he walked to the front of the house and enjoyed his coffee as the neighbor drove by. "You've got the car and I've got the second cup of coffee, you son of a bitch. That's an hour a morning, an hour an evening, two hours a day. Ten hours a week are mine and not yours. That's an extra day a week," Bart calculated. God rests for one day. Man gets two. Bart gets three.

Leisure is a rich man's game; you son of a sedan and time-share populace. As he took a slug of coffee, he didn't worry that he couldn't pay the sewage tax he raised. "Son-of-a-Rolex, see you tonight," Bart muttered to himself. His mood lightened when he saw the light of his day. His next and greatest victim of envy would be Mrs. Richmond. He could make that woman regret she was ever conceived. Bart liked to be specific. He knew he could make this woman regret the decision to rise on this particular morning. One foot, two foot: we all put on our disappointment one leg at a time or toss on a skirt for expedience.

"Good morning Mrs. Richmond." Bart raised his World Greatest Dad mug in a salute to the mother who still pushes her son in a carriage, even though he was in his thirties, same as Bart. She kept to the opposite side of the street of Bart. Always did.

Bart noted she was older today then she was yesterday. Even if it was only by one day, Bart could see it in her stringy grey hair and her skin with its multitude of thin lines looking like the belly of an albino iguana. Her eyes were dead, but they had been for years. "Old news," thought Bart.

The women at the supermarket kept the photos of the grandchildren to themselves when they saw Mrs.

Richmond approach with her box of farina and honey grahams. "Good morning," they would say. "Good morning," she would reply. The women in the beauty parlor were not so willing to contain themselves. Pictures of little Danny's and Becky's were passed from dryer to dryer. Small, proud achievements were shouted over the din. Mrs. Richmond hadn't been to the beauty parlor for years and, after that disastrous home perm, she had let herself go. Go further. Go away from where memories burn the eyes till they're mute. Her monstrous children, the mirror of her soul that came from her womb. The father claimed, "It was a virgin birth."

She didn't return Bart's salutation. That was rude. Bart saw it as a plus. Bart's heart lightened as he thought himself a bit of a mentor. Mrs. Richmond learned to hate.

"Good morning to you, Robert." Bart let ring out.

The man in the wheelchair said, "Ah, ah, ah." His baseball cap flew to the side. His eyes were blue and clouded with confusion, but his eyebrows were perfect moonlike crests. Bubbles appeared from his lips and yellow caked his nose. When Bart was a child, he liked bubbles, popped them in the air. These were different bubbles.

YOUNG BART

Thanksgiving is a time for turkeys. Everyone knows that. Year after year it's the meal, same meal, yet so few of us really knows what it's actually like to be decapitated and stuffed. And those who do, we don't let them talk about it except on talk radio and reality TV.

There is a certain amount of loyalty one should be able to expect from one's hometown. So, one should think. Shouldn't one? Who was the one who organized their Goddamn paper drives? Their Goddamn car washes. Who was it who helped the old ladies across the street no matter how they disgusted him with their humped backs and spotted flesh? The Goddamn potholed streets that you could lose a pig in. That no one had the sense to fix? Someday he would fill the potholes with old ladies. "All women are whores," he thought he heard, though it sounded like, "All women should be used for street maintenance."

Who shoveled the snow from their fucking front stoops, breaking his Goddamn back for the old bitches? Never got a fucking cent. Never got a fucking thank-you. The prick even sits in front of the post office."

Robert sits with a piece of straw hanging from the corner of his mouth. The straw sighs. It seems happy. Peace is a gift for the few and some straw.

"Bart, get me a pack of cigarettes."

"Get me a coke, Bart."

"An orange pop."

This will pass; they'll come running back to me asking for a cheese sandwich and a back scratch right up there to your left a little ways. I'll be here, just to hear them say, "I'm sorry," and I'll forgive them. They know not what they do, but were hypnotized by the outsider.

This Thanksgiving, Bart got splinters in his ass. "Let the old men laugh. I'll watch the new cheerleader. Little white skirts suspended in time, in air. Gravity on hold. Goose flesh thighs calling for warmth, warmth, warmth. Nothing can compare to that vision and light, hope for peace, pray for piece." I smiled, she frowned. "I love that kind of a woman." Around her the crowd blurred. "Why was she in a dump like this if not to meet me?" Who was that new cheerleader?

Robert flicked off his helmet after throwing his latest 90-yard pass. The black smudges under his eyes only heightened his innocence: his cheekbones higher, his clear eyes clearer. The sun glistened off his skin. Hair flattened by perspiration rested against his scalp like a newly born puppy. Any woman would hold him firmly against her tit. Ticket sales were up. The collective cheer from the bleachers reminded Bart of his rival as Robert ran over him, past him to get to the bear hug and praise of the coach. Had that ever been Bart? Had he ever been treated like an only son rather than a dirt bag, scum of the earth, my-sister-can-throw-better-than-you player?

Leading by four touchdowns, all thrown by Robert, with two minutes left, Bart entered the field with a new and interesting request. Run down the clock. Keep it on the ground. Don't fuck up, boy.

Mother fumbled her program and shook her pom-pom in the air. Father brushed the strands of crepe paper out of his face and warned her once again that she could poke his eye out with that thing. Bart was sacked. Where were his linesmen? The boys he grew up with? They went to school together. They played king of the mountain and stared at each other's pee-pees. Where were they but star-struck at the side lines? His new front line consisted of the physics class and the chess team. Only Bart knew that the pop he heard was from his knee, not the cork of an alcoholic fizzy drink that children use to celebrate in front of grownups.

Robert saluted the stands, winked at the girls and whispered, "I love you Mom and Dad." Everyone could read his lips. Bart played the game. Bart and the other team, that is. It hurt more being sacked a second time, but not as much as his team being in such a hurry to leave the huddle and not nearly as much as the agony, the pain of a smile. A smile sent over his shoulder into the face of another. She smiled at Robert. Robert smiled back. Bart was sacked again. Who is this new cheerleader, and why is she here if not to meet me?

BART

"Come on down for breakfast, lazy bones," Betty called.

Ben hoped that if he could close his eyes one more time, he'd wake in a misty glen. A place where his clothing wouldn't smell like potpourri fabric softener and breakfast meat and he wouldn't go to school every day covered in the acrid stench of bacon.

"Ouch!"

Fat little boys who stick their hands in bacon fat get burned. Betty jammed on the cold-water tap. Barry wailed like the fire engine he wanted to be when he grew up.

"What's all this racket?" Bart slammed through the storm door. Betty and Barry looked up as if caught in an incestuous moment. A blister formed on Barry's fingertips. "Let me see that." Bart took Barry's hand. Betty flipped the bacon once. Removed it from the pan. She placed the strips on two sheets of double-ply paper towels with pictures of blue ducks, blue ducks on a roll.

Bart took his suburban-sized pocketknife from his pocket, the one Betty had bought for him on Father's Day and signed the card, "Love, Barry and Ben." He examined the white-mound blisters on Barry's pinky, ring, and middle fingers. Barry whimpered.

"Stop that," Bart barked as he opened a small knife

21

and addressed Betty. "I'd think you could keep an eye on your own kid, or at least use the back burner for Christ sakes." The blisters were popped. He lifted Barry off his lap and gave him a pat on the behind. "Get a Band-Aid, son." Barry ran from the room with gloppy clown tears running down his face.

Betty heated up his coffee and gave him all of Ben's bacon. If a thank you was assumed, it was not for the substance. Bart cloaked his fear with anger and ate the cured pig and was really grateful. He needed a reason to come into the sanctuary of his own home that wasn't a retreat. A retreat from the laughter of children. Unseen children calling from the woods.

MAE & ANNA

"Who the heck can that be at this hour?" Mae clucked.
Anna barely opened her eyes to scowl, "Quiet in the
roost, Mae dear. How will I ever lay my eggs if I don't
have quiet in the roost?" Mae huffed and fluffed her
feathers as she settled back down on her fresh brown egg
while she thought to herself, "What did Anna care who
came by the hen house? They're here to see me, gather
the eggs I lay. She simply sits all day, cluck, cluck, cluck.
Not an egg in a week has she laid. Well, let it not be those
damn high school kids. Our Mrs. Schmitt has wasted her
life teaching them." Her thoughts were stopped by the
noise of children's laughter.

"Anna, help me protect my egg. It's those damn damn
damn kids out there that will steal my egg and throw it at
Mrs. Schmitt's roost. She would much rather have it soft-
boiled with a piece of dry wheat toast and some oolong
tea." Anna stood up in her nest, shaking out her spindly
legs while she filled her white meat breast with the
bracing night air.

"You vex me, Mae. You truly vex me." She flapped her
way to the hen house door. "There's no one out there.
Never was."

"I heard children."

"That's from all the eggs you lay and little chicks you

never have." Anna flew to her nest. "If our Mrs. Schmitt would borrow us a rooster, even for a week or two, you'd see me laying again."

"Really Anna, how you talk sometimes."

Anna was asleep before Mae could finish her reproach. She wished she wasn't. It's not that she didn't believe that Anna saw nothing. It was that Mae knew something was out there circling around and around like a hawk or a falcon. Even though Mae was born in an incubator in Mrs. Schmitt's high school science class, she could imagine the terrors outside from experiencing raid after raid of young men so willing to reach under her feathery bottom and feel around till they found her egg. She would nip and squawk, but to no avail. After 9:30 and Mrs. Schmitt's nightcap, they were always on their own and Anna was no help. No help at all. How the young men would waste Mae's gift, smash it under Mrs. Schmitt's window. The whites would form a circle that had lost its bounds. The yolks, Mae would track the progress of the singular yellow path as if it were a tear she could then shake from the end of her beak. At least Mae would be left to lay another day. At least she had a temporary solace when during a night she let out a "Squawk," and there it would be all over again, another egg. Anna would complain, "You could wake the dead with your carrying on." But you know when Anna's infrequent turn came to lay an egg of her own, she'd wouldn't only wake the dead, but throw them a party beside, yesirry yessirry."

"What are those children doing out there? Why don't

they get it over with?" Mae said, hearing the laughter circle closer. She closed her eyes and prayed to a large omniscient chicken with white feathers who played the piano with its beak. "Let us be done with it once and for all. I need my chicken sleep."

Four young hands raised the corrugated roof. Each grabbed a chicken around the neck.

Mae, being a chicken and not a dentist, did not know that the size of the teeth told her that the child who had her head in his mouth was only five. It didn't much matter to Mae after the child's jaw clamped down around her neck separating it from her body. When the child opened his mouth to spit her head out onto Mrs. Schmitt's neatly manicured lawn, Mae thought she could see the Moon. And what a moon it was.

FRANKIE

"Fucking glooming geeks! Real fucking glooming geeks. Son of a bitch, fucking glooming geeks!" Lester and Lestim shrank from this tiny man's enthusiasm, not knowing that Frankie had been born in the business and neither he nor his father or father before him had ever seen a real "geek." "Not a fucking drug addict or asshole college asshole willing to do anything on a dare or a dime, real cocksucking, mother-fucking geeks. Hell, they don't even have to be cocksucking." Frankie gulped for air.

New Year's and Fourth of July rarely fall on the same day. Bart had never seen a man turn more purple or imagined money so green. Bart was somehow going to get paid back for everything, and this fellow was going to see to it. "So, they're something, huh?"

Frankie sensed that some sort of negotiation had begun. He tried to turn back to his usual pallor and regretted having shown his hands, his feet, and the bald spot that he could have easily combed over. Maybe Bart hadn't noticed. Frankie wasn't face-down dead in the water yet. He knew a thing or two, or one that he'd swear on. They're gaffs. Lester and Lestim are a bunch of phony baloney gaffs. There can't be Siamese twins of different genders. Everybody knows that, everybody, everybody he knows, knows that. Ask anyone. They'll tell you they know that. That Siamese twins can't be of different genders even with a limited range of choice being from boy to girl; it will always be one or the other. It's algebraic, dealing with x and y chromosomes, ask anyone. It's as scientific as the Moon being larger than the Sun. Just look out into the sky. The truth is the truth. Ask anyone who knows a thing or two. Or ask Frankie, who knows one thing for sure. Lester and Lestim are not real. That meant Bart was greedy. That was okay in Frankie's book. He thought Bart was stupid too. He could work with that.

"This attached thing, it won't work." Frankie circled them. Lester and Lestim hovered back, fearing he would kick their tires.

Bart spit out the nub of his toothpick at the body of a chicken who had done filled her dance card and was heading home after the ball. "I've been in this business. I know this stuff forward and backward and forward." Each word was punctuated with a gesture that made him look like a special cheerleader or freshman sign student. "I know this business, I know, I know." Bart hid his worry that this strange man was about to puncture his lung with the adamant tip of his finger. "All you need is one smartass cracker, and there's always a cracker, every audience, there's always a smartass cracker. I know in every audience you'll find a smartass cracker."

Bart used his teeth to squeeze a splinter from his lip. The action hid his forthcoming smile. Frankie stood behind the twins as close as he could between them. His skin was glowing as a preliminary to him demonstrating his glorious point in a most dramatic way. "Your ass will be wiped from now to Yuma anytime that son of a bitch smartass does …" He pushed them. He pulled them.

He tried to tear them apart. They spun away into Bart's arms, each burying a face in a hip they found comforting. "Son-of-a-bitch. Son-of-a-fucking bitch. Real son-of-a-fucking bitch Siamese twins. Glooming fucking geek Siamese twins." Frankie fell to his knees and cried. His tears fell backwards, his brain pulsed. Capillaries became veins, veins rivers, in a desert, on a rainy day. A deadly rush of debris filled Frankie. Lester and Lestim felt sorry for the sobbing man, so they began their dance to cheer him up. He cried for a week. They had to call an ambulance. He was brought to the hospital. He cried there. They gave him a sedative. He cried in his sleep.

Lester and Lestim got a job. Bart bought a new shirt. Frankie was a ghost, was a legend, was who he always dreamed he could be. He was just like his grandfather.

ALBERT

The grey circles around the little boy's eyes made them call him "little old man," and his five years of life made him feel like an old man. He knew there was no Santa Claus, that children can die, and that if you swallow a tooth, it's still possible to weasel some cash from the Tooth Fairy if you put the correct words into the proper parental ear. That's right, there was no Tooth Fairy, either.

The little old man did not mind being lied to. It was their habit. He would take his disappointment and put it under the pillow where the tooth should be.

Albert took his time while he tied his shoes and dawdled as he misbuttoned his sweater so half of the collar chafed his cheek and neck. Momentarily he would be standing at the front door. His two elder brothers waited outside turning snow into slush with the impatient shuffling of their galoshes, steam pouring out their noses like rare coal furnaces.

"Albert," his mother said, calling him the name of a grandfather he never knew. "You know better than this." He would know she was right as she correctly buttoned the tip-top button, the one that keeps his neck warm, the one preventing those chest colds he was said to be prone to, the one that was so tight it would nearly make him

29

gag, but at that moment he would be so near her soft cheek. "Funny old man," she said, wanting to mush his hair, but it was parted so neatly. To mess it now would mean another half hour Albert would spend in front of the mirror in the company of his comb. She would wait for his bedtime.

"Sorry, Mom," Albert lied, as he flicked the metal buckles of his rain boots closed.

"Be careful. Watch the puddles. Call if it gets dark," came the tape loop, ring-tone voice in his head, but who's going to listen on a day when the carnival is in town? She admired her three sons as they walked down the street. It pleased her how they ranged from tall, working towards broad, to a tiny wisp formed by clothing. She wondered if a fourth had lived, if Albert would have let his sister hold his hand as they walked to the fairgrounds?

Albert had seen snow turn to slush, but when they hit the carnival it became mud. Dense mud like he'd never seen before, even in the Summer when he jumped through the backyard sprinkler, shivering as he stamped his feet and swung his toothpick arms. He had never seen rich, thick, alive mud like this. He trailed behind his brothers as if he were a little boy sea urchin following a freighter, each footstep a suction pack between him and the earth.

"Slow poke!" His brothers yelled.

Suck, suck, suck, the mud wished him to stay.

Albert stopped—stood— he swayed in concentric

circles as his brothers cursed their bad luck for not knocking down any bottles with a softball or ringing the bell with a hammer, not shooting the clown full of water till its head blew up. Albert swayed from side to side knowing that these failures were his doing. All failures were Albert's.

Tag along, tag along, behind the long-limbed brothers who once again successfully lost him in the crowd, alone and too scared to scream. He knew the number 911 and how quickly women gathered when a kid screamed, "MOM!!!" and then how quickly they look away. He is not my child. My child is safe.

Pop! His boots became unstuck and a hydroplane formed between his feet and the mud. He slid through the crowd on his tip toes, hoisted past the watchful eye of Bart Barker, hoisted up on bulging back pockets and the corners of ladies' handbags.

Thin music played through a tin speaker. Lester and Lestim whirled past the burlap curtain decorated with sun and moon, palm trees, and dandelions. Their knees stepped high as their delicate socks drooped to their ankles. The bibs of their matching sailor suits bounced up and down to the music in beat with Albert's heart. They spun as Albert had spun. In the Summer, on a picnic. In the Fall, in the leaves. In the Spring, on the blossoms. During the Winter—today—with Lester and Lestim. Around and around, till the whole drunken world whirls by the last sober child.

In the excitement, Albert tried to see their faces,

imagined open smiles with a front tooth gap and red apple cheeks. He heard their laughter from joy, not a forced-down tickle-till-he-pissed-himself laughter, over calls of, "Who's your favorite brother?"

They danced together, they were together, same age, same height as each other, as Albert. In front of grownups, they laughed and giggled, flinging their limbs like the monster who climbs out of the closet at night, but today not scary. Why?

Albert knew, without ever meeting on a playground or at Sunday school, that they would be friends. Without a word they would sit down by the blocks or fire truck and play make believe; make-believe voice, make-believe people, make-believe games. Albert would read to them what he could. Albert knew he could read better than they. He was told he was very smart. They would spell each other's names in the sand and when no one was looking, exchange little kisses.

He would be a twin again. He would know who his favorite was now: Lester and Lestim, pal and pal, Al and Al, together again. No shame in spinning till the world stands still.

Two chickens appeared from the side of the stage. Their feather flew and they clucked as they landed thump in front of the dancing children's feet. The chickens flew up, despite the metal bands around their wings, and hit the wire mess that separated the stage from the spectators. The adults swayed back in unison saying, "Whoa!" Not Albert: he watched the faces of his

32

peers shine as they danced towards the chickens, each grabbing one. Each had their own. He watched their faces shine as they grabbed their chicken by the neck and swung them over their heads so fast, he could hear the whizzing sound their feathers made against the wind.

A large hand with hairy knuckles clamped down on Albert's shoulder. "Hey kid, where's your folks? You're too young to be here without your parents. Read the sign."

"I lost my sister."

"You won't find her here.," Bart said, and he was right.

Lifted out of the tent. He woke from a dream; the stillborn, reborn.

"Albert, where were you? We had to call Mom, you know, and now she's coming to pick us up. Boy, is she pissed at you." Albert concealed his little old man smile, even as his brothers continued with their threats of no supper, no summer, no television, no air, no water, no light. Albert acted scared, because in a way he did love them, even though they weren't his favorites, and wanted them to be happy. Yelling at Albert made them happy, so be it. It didn't matter now that it was a fair fight. No longer two against one.

No one remembered where Albert's blue baby doll came from, but everyone remembered how Albert loved his blue baby doll. A ragged, old stuffed toy that was always in the big-boy bed at night and, in the morning, dragged from place to place, even if place to place meant nothing but where Albert was. No ceremony was performed when it was put away. No date was marked on the calendar to note its exile, put on the shelf rather than to the comfort of sleeping. "You're no longer a baby anymore." Anyway, it was missing an ear and the pupil had left its left eye. It was broken. It couldn't be fixed.

Tonight, Albert listened for everyone to sleep. The television was turned off. The brothers stopped their fighting. Down in the front hall closet, Albert takes a belt from his father's trench coat. He straps himself back-to-back with his little blue baby doll. On the tippy top of his tippy toes, he unchains the door. The weather is colder than this afternoon. Snow lightly falls. Melts as it hits the salted walk. Tonight, Albert can dance in the snow with his baby Allison, three minutes his junior, little blue baby doll, little blue baby.

BART

The clock switched from 8:56 to 8:57 as Mayor Bart entered his office. He was always grateful when he arrived before his never-punctual secretary, Cindy.

In the outer office he stood on the fatigue-free mat, counting slowly in his head as he drew large scoops of coffee out of the can: one, two, three ... ten. He thought about the first cup, sitting back with his feet on the desk; jacket slung over the back of his leather recliner, fresh newspaper warm and virginal, lying prone on the desk.

Cindy would arrive during that time, after the sports, before the op-eds. The familiar odor of the coffee, which she buys freshly ground at the supermarket on Tuesdays during her lunch hour to make up for being late on Monday, the familiar odor of the coffee grounds would toss her into a flurry—late again. Unclasping her sweater, she would scurry into Bart's office with a story about a car battery or overflowing toilet, being kidnapped by aliens with overflowing toilets. The flying saucer had a flat. Cindy's stories put a half-smile on Bart's face.

At dinner, Betty would try to get Bart to open up about work by asking why he kept that ding dong who runs around like a chicken with her head cut off.

Cindy comes from a big family. She was somewhere in the middle of too many boys, who were now all married and had too many boys of their own. Bart needed the votes.

Cindy would bring him his second cup as she brought the mail. Then she'd sit at her desk in the reception area, taking a deep breath as she played back the answering machine, transposing all the messages on to individual slips of pink paper, double checking the phone numbers with her Rolodex. She would then prioritize the messages in order of importance. Cindy was connected to the sewer and lived on a well-paved road. She would deliver the messages in time for Bart's third cup of coffee.

Bart would hand back the correspondence along with a verbal barrage of orders. The forthcoming buzz of the intercom would be met with a "What!" Left alone in his office, Bart would part the messages, recycling the bottom half, phoning the top slips. Bart would phone these people in an easygoing manner that inspired confidence. He felt he sounded like somebody's father.

Cindy waited to catch the phone lights in mid-blink, then used Bart's fourth cup of coffee to slip in a question about the correspondence she was typing at 20 wpm. Some things she needed to double-check, or never quite understood to begin with.

Bart would tilt back in his chair. He let her see the smile he had saved up for her. Good ol' Cindy, he knew what she was up to. That look scared her so that her bones would start to fuse.

Years later, during the autopsy, the doctors were very

puzzled at this phenomenon. It wasn't cancer that caused the pain—the doctors never met up with Bart's smile. Cindy was lucky. The ear to ear would have killed her outright. It might have killed Bart as well.

If Bart would listen to what the hell Cindy asked, he might have been able to answer those daily questions, instead of twirling in his recliner and treating the citizen on the other end of the optic fibers as an equal. After that encounter, everything else was downhill.

The red plaid thermos was washed and scrubbed, and cup five and six accompanied Bart as he drove the taupe town car with a seal on the front door to supermarket openings and to model daycare centers where he would sit and read antidrug messages to undernourished children with some shiny-faced skinny high school kid wearing second generation pocket protectors, snapping Bart's picture with the third generation Leica camera.

Bart would give him a slap on the back and tell him to send the pictures to his office. The kid would smile and take another picture—snap. Bart hoped the friendly pat would set off his asthma. The next week the kid would bring in two mint copies of the high school gazette, hoping for a personal delivery only to be told that Mr. Barker was in conference. Someday the kid would learn what cup #7 can do to a man.

There would always be a concerned citizen or chamber of commerce to fill the afternoon. They would be cups #9 and #10. Then Cindy would ask, "Fresh pot?"

She stood on the mat counting one to ten plus one for

the pot as she scooped out the coffee. Bart would have cup #1. After all, it was a fresh pot.

Bart bent over to pick up the packet of Sweet'N Low, a luxury he indulged in during his afternoon breaks. He felt that old football injury flare up in his knee. He was old—not old, not young. Age wasn't a cold he could get over. As he unlocked his knee, he looked around the office, realizing that he had not accomplished anything more with his life than Robert had.

ROBERT

If Norman Rockwell was to paint, which was what Norman Rockwell did—if he was painting yesterdays, todays, and tomorrows—it would be the Richmond's he painted. The Richmond's in their car, driving to church. The Richmond's having a barbecue. The Richmond's in their RV: "Look how beautiful the canyon is." Spreading joy to every Denny's they pass. Their dog scoops its own poop. It never humps a stranger's leg. Their individual perfection creates a greater whole.

Robert was wearing a red flannel shirt, half would call it new, half might say worn. He folded it up to his elbows. It never slid down, held in place by the muscles of his forearm, the arm that held the beer can. His Levi's were slightly faded to the right of his crotch. Everyone pretended not to stare. His cheeks were red like apples. Bart burped and reached for his girl's tit to steady himself that night at the Richmond's party for the victors.

The parents remained upstairs, friendly yet unobtrusive. As respectful as servants. They read good books and smiled a lot at what those kids call music, and what a mess they would make, but how as a family they would clean it all up tomorrow, and how quickly they would complete their task working together, laughing, singing.

Bart wore a girl on his drunk to keep himself steady. His arm lay heavily on her shoulder. A victory party is, of course, a time for merriment. Bart was a little more drunk than merriment required. Bart had wanted a day to remember forever, and he did not want it to be from the pain in his knee he would feel every time there was a chance for rain. He felt he had a special right. He kissed his girl, sliding his tongue through her lips, but not beyond the great wall of pearly whites. He pumped out his right cheek with his own tongue. The girl's tongue stayed slumbered in the chastity of her teeth. He hoped everyone was looking. Feared no one cared.

In the corner of the basement rec room, designed for adolescents with friends, was his vision, the vision of a girl, a woman, a woman child, a vision of a wet dream that Bart wasn't going to wait to have. He imagined her as he saw her: "Go, Team, Go." Men liked her. Woman liked her. The dog liked her, sitting with his head on her lap, its large brown eyes, the scar on the bottom of his chin received in the heat of battle with a cat. He listens to her breathing, like all the rest around her.

Bart watched her talk, laugh, listen. She was perfect. He heard the sound of air slowly seeping out of a balloon. It was him. Nancy slipped away to discuss her newest eye shadow and the texture of Bart's tongue. That's okay, thought Bart, he'd boff her later. But now was the time to stare, stare and leer and prey to God that she believed in love at first sight, or at least that he could sell that concept to her. Sex was oozing out of every one of his pores. That his manly scent would cause her to leave the throngs of twits, kick the dog, and come running into his arms. They'd dance crotch to crotch, not stopping when the music did. He'd take her right there, like slow music, with the rising and falling of the orchestra backing him up. Not that he needed any backing up.

She seemed to be alone, not paying any real interest to anyone—that's good—but who is she? Where did she come from? Bart put his pelvis in gear and started his move—never a blink, never a shudder. She rose to her feet. Her lips damp, eyes glazed. The dog fell to the floor, favored itself. Bart trembled as her mouth moved. Then she spoke. "Robert."

Robert came up from behind him, a tray of cheese puffs and dough-wrapped dogs his mother popped out of the oven, no problem at all. "How's the knee, Bart? You should ice it for the first 24 hours." Bart recoiled from the pat pat pat on his back back back.

"I'll do that." Bart turned away, running towards the back door. He was puking over the ceramic geranium pot when he heard Robert call after him, "Hey, Bart, you've met Diane, my sister?"

YOUNG BART

Diane, the word lay on him like a warm blanket. Diane, wrapping him in a pleasant haze of birth and the bright light of death; Diane, Diane, Diane. Her soft hair running through his hands. Diane. Diane. Her eyes that sparkle with acceptance. My Diane. Whirling through the soul. Hello, Diane. The smoke alarm sounded from the kitchen. He was born.

The toaster had jammed. The white bread turned black. Bart knew windows would be open and towels swung over heads. The observer would think his parents were performing a joyous Greek dance. Bart knows the disappointment of burnt toast.

Bart rolled over in his bed and tried to fall back to sleep. He closed his eyes, Hello, Diane. His father yelled, "Dumb bitch!" at his mother. He pulled the blanket up over his head. A dish was broken. Bart turned over to catch the dream that was quickly running in the wrong direction: Diane. The front door slammed.

Bart got out of bed, took two aspirin, and finished the coffee his father left behind. He was very conscious of being so adult, which is why he wore that flannel bathrobe his mother had gotten him during his last bout of flu. It looked like a child's, though to Bart, it was his grandfather's. As he added some milk and sugar to the coffee, he wondered where do dreams go. The milk was sour. That was all the answer Bart needed. Mother turned the toaster upside down and shook the dead bread ash into the white porcelain sink.

BART

Bart chucked his bolt action shotgun into position. "Who's there? What's that noise?" Bart huskily whispered though his back screen door. His words greeting the night air with a cloud of mist. As he stepped out into the cold, moist night, the frost-covered blades of grass stunned the bottom of his bare feet, causing the hair on his toes to stand on end.

"Show yourself." There was no fear in Bart's voice, he thought.

Laughing nymphs romping with the moonlight. Scraps of clothing adorned their bodies: torn khakis, a plaid dress. They could not be more than four or five. Back-to-back they celebrated the celebration they celebrated. They danced.

Bart remembered how Chuck would come to the door and ask if Bart could come out and play. He doesn't remember the answer.

Could Bart come out and play?

Bart recognized the flaying headless chicken bodies they carried in their hands. It was Mae and Anna, two of Ol' Miz Schmitt's laying hens. He identified them by their feathery brown and white bottoms they liked to haughtily wave in the air every time Bart walked past their coop. It wasn't like he ever saw an egg from them.

The children poured the blood down their faces and into the mouths. Their hair was caked with previous meals that created the look of red/brown dregs around their cherub faces.

Once the blood was swallowed, they sat down back-to-back to fling the chickens over their shoulder and hit the other twin on the head. The red stalk-like feet of Mae and Anna seem to tickle as they tap, tap, tapped their heads, breaking up the dried remains of a lunch or breakfast or last night's supper. It was when back-lit by the moonlight that Bart could see why they sat back-to-back rather than front-to-front, which is how he would if he wished to hit someone on the head with a dead chicken. A trunk of flesh ran from child to child from the base of the spine to where their buttocks met Bart's sod. It seemed thicker than the children's waist and harder than oak. "Strange," Bart thought as the children tossed clumps of feathers into the air. They laughed at the falling down.

Chuck came running out of the house, shotgun in hand. "What the hell is that?" Bart let off two rounds in the air. The children ran. Lights flicked on from neighbor window to neighbor window. Lester dropped her chicken, Mae. She wanted to stop to pick it up, but Lestim was running her forward, moving her closer and closer, running in tornado fashion into the safety of the woods.

"It's those damn high school kids," Bart said, as he thanked his shotgun and lowered it to his side. They'd be safe there. Bart felt relieved when he saw them disappear into the forest fringe. Run, little children. You'll be safe runaway children, good runaway children, happy runaway children.

"Damn kids," Chuck said as he slung his shotgun over his shoulder and disappeared back into his house.

"Damn kids," Bart murmured back as if to say, "Good night, sweet dreams."

"Bart, is that you?" Betty slid open the upstairs window. How he wished to cock his gun and shoot again. "It's nothing, Betty, just a couple of coyotes or those damn kids."

"Damn kids." Betty closed the window and hid her desire to have a body temperature of 98.6 laying beside her. She could always manage to snuggle up to his body, especially after he was asleep. There was a lesser chance of a violent jolt pushing her away.

Bart aimed his empty shotgun at the Moon and pulled the trigger. He saw the buckshot pierce the Moon's membrane and the air gush out, causing it to zig-zag frantically across the night sky. The Moon fell exhausted into Bozer's old pen. By tomorrow morning, as Bart would circle his house with his morning coffee in this "World's Greatest Dad" mug, it would already be gone. Some early rising Blue Jay would have been around and picked up the tattered Moon for a part of its nest, along with a piece of string and some dried grass.

BEN

Where Bart and Betty found the name Ben, no one knows. He would be called Ben or Benji or Benny or Douchebag, but that had nothing to do with the name Ben. One day at school some of his classmates were doing what classmates do best, humiliation and torture, but when the teacher turned around, what name did she ring out? BENJAMIN! No one had ever heard his name Benjamin. Being new, it was set up for ridicule during recess, when order and law stepped aside for a coffee and cigarettes, healthy snacks and naps, do not slip into that void. Benjamin Barker, Benjamin Barker, just a name, became a taunt. This shouldn't happen. It wasn't like his name was Peter or Dick or Lisa or Sue.

After school, Ben ran crying home. Betty was in the kitchen, cleaning the aluminum or cooking vegetables. Ben ran in and, with anger through his tears, cried, "Why did you ever call me Benjamin?" He ran up to his room and slammed the door.

This aggressiveness could only be displayed when it was just him and his mother. If he ran, he had three minutes with his mother for himself alone, before his brother arrived home. I mean his mother had another son and an absent husband to loathe. Ben was an amateur. Which is why it should be that mothers eat their young. She can only deal with so much. He was called down for dinner, but did not eat. When asked by his mother had anything exciting happened, he said, "Nothing." Ben began to wonder if she even heard, since she wasn't listening. Since Bart's disappearance, Betty was only listening to her internal monologue that said bills, bills, bills, or bastard, bastard, bastard. Betty asked the routine question of Barry, who went into his escapades, which were similar to yesterday's. More nothing with more words. Ben wished he could be like Barry, but not stupid or cruel or anything else that made Barry Barry.

Teasing, alas, has a varied span. It can be born and die in 24 hours or can live to be the age of a great turtle. Or, like the 17-year locust: it can lie dormant for years only to make blindly clear its return.

Well, Benjamin rose like a Phoenix and would not fade. Since children shouldn't play with matches, it lacked a ball of fire to consume itself. As bad as things were during homeroom and recess and after-school, Ben had no idea that things were about to get worse. He couldn't even get home in time to yell at his mother because he had to stop on the way to be beaten up. If he owned a watch, he could set his calendar by it. By the time he got home, Barry was at his mother's elbow, telling her of his escapades, which were very similar to yesterday's, while licking the remaining icing out of the can. Ben didn't stay. "Run," he thought he heard his mother say, though she hadn't moved her lips.

He knew he would hear the same story at dinner. When he went to his room and closed the door (not a slam but a statement), Ben thought he heard his mother say, "Benji, is that you?" It might as well have been a squirrel in the attic.

Ben sat at dinner and said nothing, ate nothing. He was afraid he would vomit when he would be punched in the stomach tomorrow. Then he would be called gross. His parents hadn't named him Vomit, Puke, or Mucus. Why didn't he feel gratitude for that?

What is luck? Was it good luck that Gregory Simon's big brother was home from college because he was suspended for removing the genitals from the male frog and putting them in the female, (in the process making quite a mess and starting a fire somehow)? And whose luck was it that Gregory Simon's big brother liked the old-time English history and musical theatre? Was it the rats he dissected?

Gregory Simon's parents were talking about the missing Mr. Barker. When Gregory mentioned his schoolmate Benjamin Barker, it sent Gregory Simon's brother off—spending the next two hours singing. Their mother found a place of emptiness in her head that would make a Buddhist monk say, "Holy Shit, lady. How did you do that?" His father worked out the math in his head, about how much the Barkers owed them. After a fair amount of addition and subtraction, Father blurted out, "They're killing us." Mother woke from enlightenment to ask who. When Father said, "Barker,"

Gregory Simon's brother knew just what he had to do. Today, vengeance would be on the Simons' side.

Gregory Simon's brother gave himself an intermission, a glass of water, and a pee break. When he flicked the lights on and off, they thought there was a brown out. Or, "Damn, another fixture to replace." Gregory Simon's big brother sang at church in a beautiful soprano voice that happened to fall into a bass just in time for a high school production of Sweeney Todd and the hormonal cue for the darkness of thought to fall upon Gregory Simon's older brother. The stars are aligned. The Moon is full. Does darkness rise from the East or the West? Or is it the light that missed its cue? Is that why Gregory Simon's older brother happened to be paying some attention when Gregory said the name "Benjamin Barker" during the Simons' dinner time relating? Was it for Gregory's sake, or for the sake of Gregory's sister, that Gregory Simon's older brother went into a long, vivid description of Benjamin Barker, a.k.a. Sweeney Todd, a dead man famous for killing other men, harvesting the nature fruits of the body flesh, as a nutritional source? More than bologna has a first name. Gregory Simon's older brother didn't put it quite that way. Gregory Simon's older sister thought it was gross. Gregory Simon agreed. His heart lightened. His eyes sparkled. Tomorrow was going to be his day, and maybe even the day after, and the day after next. Oh, God, please make me popular with the older boys but not the girls, yuck.

Battle weary, Ben woke up late. The problem with

waking up after Barry was that Barry would then wake you up. Not, "Good morning, brother, rise and shine, lazy bones," but he would sit on your face and fart. Some kids could burp on command. Some can make fart sounds with their hand and arm pits. Some could turn their eyelids inside out. Let us just say Barry was a prodigy. If Ben overslept, a P.O.W. humiliation would be a gin and tonic after tennis, compared to Barry's morning services.

Barry ran to school. He wasn't allowed to beat up his own brother in public, only in the privacy of his own home. And for Barry, violence of the fist held less interest than the mass destruction a joystick can bring. The 'smarts' the fist learned is "don't". Unless you want to be punched back. So, Barry went off to school to watch someone else beat up somebody else's brother. Maybe someday he would call himself a pacifist.

Gregory waited out front; he'd hardly slept, his head so full of imagined glory. The first bell went off and there was no Ben. How could a little douchebag like Benjamin Barker do this to him?

Ben was sent to the principal's office for tardiness, which makes sense, to punish someone who doesn't want to be in school by taking him out of class. The silence of the principal's office was the bitter cold before it cracks the snow. The secretary eyed Ben with loathing and disgust, but it was nothing personal. It was a habit she picked up from working with too many children as she tick-tocked out till retirement. She treated all children that way. She was a woman who hated well. It was a perfect place for her to work. Everyone should be entitled to a little happiness and deserving of a little misery. Being able to accomplish both simultaneously, she had time to work on her bucket list.

Ben sat on a chair in the principal's office. The back of the chair came to over his head. Stretching his feet, he could not reach the floor. From this point, he got smaller.

He hoped the afterschool detention room would be quiet, so he could concentrate on how we would explain it to his mother. Since his father disappeared, anytime he spoke to her, it was always in the form of an apology for embarrassment caused to the Barker name. How to tell her the problem was the name he had given him, Benjamin, the name of the father's father's, father. Ben wondered why they couldn't think of anything new. There were 15 boys in class, and they all had different names, though five of them were Mark and another three Steve.

Gregory Simon was sitting through mathematics drawing pictures of slashed thoughts and writing "Benjamin Barker" over and over. If it had not been for the twisted faces of the murdered, you would have thought he was in love.

The lunch hour came upon Ben quicker than he would have wished. For Gregory Simon, the time was an eternity. Ben entered the playground a shattered knight. His arrows were old, the feathers worn. He had no weapon for protection or God for defense, only an egg salad sandwich, a box drink, and a snack cake.

By then, Gregory had shown his pictures and told his

tales. He jumped off the high wall that only the tall boys could climb and looked Ben straight in the eyes and said, menacing, "Benjamin Barker," then walked away. That was the only taunt. He walked away with a satisfied swagger. His seed was planted, and the climate was good for growth. The playground was abuzz.

Ben, a lone gunman waiting for an ambush, not knowing where it would come: A sniper on the swing set? An assassin on the sliding board? "Do not forsake me, oh, my darlin'." The girls took their multi-colored chalk, but today wasn't a day for hopscotch. They outlined each other's bodies till it looked like a scene from a mass murder. One of the little girls poured her punch on the ground hoping it would resemble blood. It only blended with the asphalt and ran the chalk lines before she had time to say, "Look." She ruined everything. It would be her turn next week.

Could it be the same Benjamin Barker who mourned for dying birds and cringed at his brother's amputation of spider legs? Could he, Benjamin Barker, be pushed to a brutality and violence that he was also a victim of? In the crapper, Ben heard the boys telling the tales of their new vulgar hero, Benjamin Barker, slitting throats, slicing hearts out to watch the last beat. Dicing the innocent into workable sizes. Ben sat on top of the toilet. His egg salad repeated. The smoke and the heat made him feel very old. He sat there till detention. Then, he sat there.

That night no one asked about his day, and Barry made no comment. Bastard, bastard, bastard. The dining room table was short one bastard. Benjamin Barker missed his father.

Ben looked at his meal and thought of diseased Victorian flesh. He could not eat. Barry asked for seconds. Ben could not sleep. His name came to haunt him. When he closed his eyes, his victims dripped their blood on his face. Betty was surprised to find her baby boy bathing at three in the morning. She wrapped him in a towel and said, what a good boy. "Shh, don't wake your brother." "Run..." how did she speak without moving her lips? Mother closed her eyes.

Ben's face was red from rubbing his eyes, red from not sleeping, his nose, red from crying. Walking to school, he would hear that sound that children like to make when someone's throat is being slit, though in reality it doesn't cause that much noise. But they haven't learned that yet. This isn't high school.

Their faces all had tongues dripping out of their mouths and fingers running along their throats. He wrote M.I.C.H.A.E.L on the top of the page. Michael, that's a nice name, Michael Barker. He said it out loud. The secretary eyed him with disgust and loathing—his feet never touched the floor. "Paris," she wrote, after marriage and before Grand Canyon. Her feet were planted.

His eyes saw the blood. His ears heard the sound. His body was not clean. He spent dinner in the bathroom. Betty called a doctor. He sent a bill—biLL, BILL. No, Bill would not do.

Days flowed to the nightmares that entered on the wagging tail of light. He woke to see his teddy bear lying on his back with stuffing coming out the slit in its neck.

If he could do this to Teddy, who next? His brother, his mother? Maybe he'd already killed his father. No, it couldn't be his mother. He must save her from this Benjamin Barker who was so much a stranger.

He was scrubbed and ready for school on time, for a change. Betty never wondered why her son's arms hung on to her neck a little longer than what they considered appropriate for a child that age.

Ben never went to school. He went out to the woods that, at that time, separated the two towns with two tax structures and two totally different ideas about the quality of education. Separating the forest was a stream on which makeshift bridges were built for late-night attacks on personal property.

One of the shaky bridge structures had collapsed and, fortunately for Ben, had become a dam. The puddle it created Ben dubbed a lake. Ben spent the day in the muck, washing away sins he would never commit. His skin turned blue. Before he passed out, he thought he heard the name one last time: Benjamin Barker.

BART

Men dress in dirt and dungarees, play familiar old songs that are passed from father to son.

The waitress' eyes swelled with tears that burst their barrier at her memories, exposed through the rhyming refrain. Bart didn't like women's tears. Women's tears were like the green men with long heads and bug eyes who came to see his show.

Women's tears brought them big tips and fatherly hugs. Women's tears gave them power. High octane, zero to sixty, onto your lap, into your pockets. Women's tears made for the quick sham. They caught easy marks for an easy sell.

Secretions from a woman's body should be limited by law to vagina, nose, and ears, and he wished like hell someone would do something about the ears. Though ear wax did give him a certain insight in moments of darkness masked as intimacy. When truth is wiped from the bottom of the shoes and locked outside on the welcome mat.

Women expecting something warm and friendly at the end of the night have that habit of doing a "one two" cotton swab number between applying mascara and perfume. The woman knowing, of course, that she is mentally superior to all men. Therefore, the first thing he wishes to do is suck out her brain to make her an equal.

Proceed with caution. An Olympic diver going for the gold. In her plastic handbag with the initials of some French man, she keeps a set of large white cards with the individual numbers, one-to-ten, ready to share her rating with the world. She marks the Olympians as the overzealous amateurs they are.

Sure, Bart knows women like that. They're the ones he calls bitches in the morning, somewhere between using her toothbrush and taking his shower.

Then there are those women with the sweet potato fields. Wild potatoes on the hills, in the valleys, defying gravity, no famine to create generations of cops, have flowered and gone to seed, then flowered again farther afield deep into the placed called the Valley Of Ear.

The exploratory surgery should start early in the evening. Room to maneuver and time to fuck before Mr. Sandman takes you both away from the grind of the week or just that day. How beautiful she was, in a foolish sort of way. Life was as a surprise to her as it was to a child, a shy child, a scared child. Curious, naive, and terrified of both sides of the hairbrush, she returned from the ladies' room, cautious not to trip on the floor whose tiles seemed to leap with her expectation. She hadn't expected to meet such a nice man. She smiled a smile just for Bart, yet was concerned for the filth that crossed her mind, that scurried like rats through the speculation of bystanders.

Her geranium soap smelled nice. She was warm;

thighs looked comfortable. Superman could see the scars, the stretch marks, the tell-tale sign of the failed attempt of a false ideal. He kissed her and told her she was loved. Bart was surprised that he tasted blood. And thought maybe her blushing was not caused by his flattery but was caused by the knowledge that she had deafened herself in one ear. He held her hand and found the nail that had done the damage. He kissed her hand to get a whiff of something as inviting as clean white sheets on a cool night and as unexpected as a candy bar bought by a stranger and placed in your grocery bag. It looked like sweet, sweet, sweet potato pie.

Bart will repeat, "I love you," before he goes home and gives his children a chicken to bite the head off of.

DIANE

Diane held her book so tight it became a Wagnerian shield. "But it's so nice not to go with a date, *per se*. You get to talk to everyone. It's friendly. No one's feelings get hurt. Don't you think? Will you be there?"

"No." Bart leaned his head back to get some cool from the metal locker since he was losing his. "The real fun comes after the dance. I've got a car."

"Thank you anyway." Diane didn't know why she should suddenly be so thirsty.

He played with the two hairs that were to become his moustache. "Come on, what are you afraid of?"

"That we'll be out way past my curfew. I don't think it's fair to keep my parents up worrying."

"Leave the dance early."

"Robert ..."

"What? He won't have anyone to talk to, or he might have a good time without his sister hanging around." Bart knew one was a lie and the other the truth. He wanted Diane to tell him which one.

"I have to go ... my next class?"

Bart stood tall. "I didn't hear no bell."

Diane cringed as something inside of her was sparked that she didn't recognize. Was she liking a bad boy or bad grammar? "Well, we know it's about to ring." Was there more? "Don't we?"

As she pranced past him, Bart mumbled, "Cockteasing, cold-hearted bitch," which was drowned out by the bell. He went to biology.

Mr. Leonard was writing on the board as Diane took her seat. Not in the first row with the know-it-alls with nothing else to do with their lives but piss off the rest of the world with their superior intelligence. She didn't sit in the back with the I-don't-cares with their short attention spans, their attitudes in the latest style and color. She sat in the second row, one seat in, like a sunset at the beach.

Having a master's degree and only teaching accelerated mathematics, Mr. Leonard didn't know how to deal with failure and favorites; he merely knew correct and wrong, wrong, wrong. "Solve the equation," he said.

Diane wrote in her notebook $2x=6$. Bart didn't seem like such a bad boy. He tried too hard, that's all. 2 divided by 2, that doesn't mean he'll always, 6 divided by 2, be like that. He's the kind of boy to keep you out past curfew, equals. Mom and Dad trust me, they won't really mind. If he washed a bit more, I'm sure he'd have skin like Robert's. Though he's not like Robert. Bart would drive fast with the lights off; he would drive without his seat belt on. Equals, Bart would eat Chinese food in the dark.

"Diane!" Mr. Leonard repeated, "What is the value of x?"

The value of x? Diane should know the value of x.

"Good morning, Miss Richmond, sorry to disturb you," Mr. Leonard teased. The class laughed as teach found another victim.

"Jarrod, are you with us?"

The value of x? Failure opened its dark, dank mouth to Diane and released its triumphant laugh, HA! She leaped from its reach and towards the well-marked path of long division.

"Three!" she said, but it was too late. The answer was known and no one wanted to hear it a second time. No, Bart would not do at all.

YOUNG BART

On a cold, rainy, adolescent night, when the kids call you names, the teacher fails your test, and your parents forget they once made love to conceive you, you go to bed early with your shoes still on, and in the mirror of your dream, behind you and in front of you, turn around and look, there is Robert Richmond, not Bob, never Robby. There is Robert Richmond's silken chest, with pecs larger than the schoolgirl's bosom. Tense little brown nipples, beauty marks to highlight the rib cage like a grand staircase, dancing fingers over ribbed stomach muscles. A geyser of hair teases the belly button that is slightly protruding, reminding him of how he loves his mother. Lightly haired legs strong enough to wrap around a body and break it in two. The arms look good in a T-shirt, leaving a slight tan mark that's not altogether unsexy. The hands rushing the suds though his thick hair, down his back, and swoop off the curve of his ass. His penis lies flaccid, unexcited by all around him.

Bart hated the locker room and the single-mindedness with which Robert put on his socks. Always clean, always white, with two or three colored stripes on top, as if each pair was worn only once then passed on to an old lady to wear against her bosom as a fetish. Someday Bart would say, "I never dream. Never had to."

FRANKIE

Frankie skirts around the industrial streets on the outskirts of town to avoid anything that might resemble trouble. In his usual seat, on the beaded back massager, he drives the once-yellow school bus now, painted in shades of Playdoh. The banner that hangs over the opaque windows reads, "Prince Raphael's Odditorium," and underneath in small letters, "Fun For the Whole Family."

Prince Raphael, or Ralph, the anglicized version of that name which a young boy first heard from a doctor who made him cough and listened to his heart before he pushed him along on his way to the ferry that would lead him off Ellis Island; Raphael was Frankie's paternal grandfather.

Raphael picked up his satchel and his mother's bag that held her best dress, button shoes, and the wool coat she used to wear, holding it close around her neck in a feeble attempt to keep out the cold Atlantic winds. Raphael was missing her as he walked down the darkened streets of a budding slum called the Lower East Side, looking for a place to stay, something to eat, a road paved with gold. His mother had been the one with a plan.

A hysterical woman stalled his self-pity. She ran from

the back of the tenement and would have thrown herself in front of the Junkman's cart, but for her husband grabbing her, locking his arms around her. Though larger than he, she was softer. The husband abandoned his body weight and felled her. They lay in the gutter amidst the vegetable rinds and animal excretions. She cursed and he cried, burying his sobs in her breast.

The language they bawled was more foreign than the English spoken in Raphael's new country, though he could understand the meaning, knowing firsthand the sting of Satan and the indulgence of the Lord.

Raphael expected something worse than death, desertion, and being alone in a foreign land with only an extra pair of knickers and a change of linens when he walked down the alley between the tenement buildings where the couple had sprung from. Over his head two woman gossiped, their tongues left comet trails in a swirl of coal smoke. They stopped to watch him pass.

A cat spat out a chicken bone, hiss—run—into the basement to lick its paws and watch a young girl scrape a sheet along the ridges of a washboard, a girl who will never know satellite communications, the polio vaccine, or soap that smells like evergreens. She will never know evergreen trees either, tall, fresh pines on crisp winter days blanketed in pure white snow. She did not look up as Raphael passed.

Behind the building was a little patch of land. A wooden shack sat in the corner of the yard. One side open, had no wall. The roof slanted back to keep out the rain. He'd seen these before, not at the farm he remembered from the time he still had a father. When he could still see the sky and run with abandon, but from a time just before now. The poor city farmers struggling to keep a goat to provide milk and cheese, or a couple of laying hens for when the work dried up, or the land. He remembered the woman for whom his mother had cleaned, kept some chickens in a shed, like this, till the neighbor's dog found out. He heard the widow's threats and accusations from behind the bolted door of the room he shared with his mother. He remembered how quiet the gnarly widow got when she saw the black snout covered with white feathers. The quiet before the tempest. When he heard the shot, he was glad to be alive. He would miss the occasional egg, but then again there would be no barking to disturb his sleep, only his mother's prayers and tears.

Raphael heard a thin cry as he maneuvered through the garbage thrown from the top floors to make his way to the manger. A goat lay freshly dead. The memory of breath remained in her eyes. Her newborn kid searched for balance in the bloody straw, wet from birth. If the kid could imagine the warm lick of a mother's tongue or the milk she held inside, he would have regrets. He had none. The baby goat shook the placenta off his eyes and cried from hunger. Raphael knelt next to the dead mother and forced the milk from her udder, enough for the two heads of the kid.

Raphael left his mother's suitcase in exchange for the

new goat, but he kept his mother's coat that was not warm enough for the north winds. It would have to do for the baby Raphael carried from the tenement.

Down the street he traded the silver picture frame that held the portraiture of him on the lap of his mother and a broad-shouldered man who had been his father, for a pushcart. Then he traveled uptown with his two-headed goat he had named Kaufman, after the man who had made him cough and let him know he had a heart.

BART

Bart put his arm carefully around the Older Miz Schmitt, who held her decapitated chicken, Mae, so close to her that the congealing blood was performing a slow drip from her elbow as if it was a leaky faucet. Not yet worth the money to call the plumber. Older Miz Schmitt wiped the tears from her cheek. Their heavy salt content and the sheer abundance of them made her face itch and sting. She left behind a smear of blood; Indian child plays with war paint, but with no one left to fight.

Bart patted her gently on the shoulder: once, twice. Older Miz Schmitt looked up at him. He thought he could feel a faint tremble, and that some of the tears might be partially caused by some reminiscences of him as a lad. That was till she said, "You haven't changed a bit, Bart Barker. There always was a smart aleck look in your eyes. Even comforting your favorite teacher, one who's known you since you pee-peed in your pants, you can't get away from looking at yourself." She turned quickly away. Mae's blood sprinkled the rhododendron leaves.

"We're a small town with limited resources. We're doing everything we can, Grace." She was the only Grace he knew. It was an old name, and like other old names, it was going extinct along with Faith, Joy, and Hope.

"It is the small minds that have ruined everything. It's always been your home too, Barton. Don't you care?"

Bart couldn't help but stare at Mae's long neck draped over his teacher's arm. "But I swear to you, Bart Barker, you do this one thing right, you see to it that justice is brought, and I'll reevaluate what a louse I'm sure you are, bless that Betty, and maybe even light a candle." She took a deep breath and found a poise-school posture in her decalcifying bones. "Excuse me, I have arrangements to make for an old friend."

Bart never noticed her dignity as she walked across the yard, back to her home where friends were gathering with coffee cake, condolences, and lemonade. He mumbled, "Crazy old bitch," as he unraveled the garden hose to wash down the lawn and shrubbery where Mae had drip, drip, dripped her last drop.

When he heard the giggle, he saw the dirty faces of the two blond-haired children peer at him though the basement. He was glad they hadn't laughed when Older Miz. Schmitt was there. The presence of blood-coated Siamese twins in his basement would have been difficult to explain, though not impossible, given Bart's ability to authoritatively shrug. He watered the geraniums that had been doing very well, and another rhododendron bush because it needed it and he had the hose out. He curled up the garden hose, piling circle upon circle with the same precision as a fire brigade but minus the manpower. Then he opened the metal doors of the storm cellar. The children needed a bath.

FRANKIE

Frankie tapped his foot that rested on the clutch, while humming along with the grinding of the gears. He was always eager for the next town and the routine and the cash that went along with it. He festooned the exterior of the bus in the once-colorful, faded banners, placing his barker stand by the front of the once-colorful bus and setting the tattered velvet ropes, which the people had to pass through for the most amazing, spectacular view of Prince Raphael's Most Amazing Spectacular Odditorium. Never before, never again, something such as this will you see. When Frankie works his pitch through the bullhorn, he lowers the tone of his voice to create a commanding resonance rather than a weasel's squeal.

Kaufman's breath grew labored as Raphael pushed his cart through the vegetable vendors and knife grinders: young men running to pray, running to steal. Through the coat, Raphael could see the baby's one heart leap and two heads bob along with the ruggedness of the cobblestone way. He tried to steal a pail of milk, but found a twisted arm and blackened eye instead. He thought of the young mothers who nursed their infants on the boat ride over as he ran his hand over his flat chest. Two tongues lapped water from his cupped hands.

As night fell, Raphael stopped walking. There was no

rainbow to find gold at, and there was no bread or milk. He pushed his cart into an alleyway, crawled into the back with his goat. Their hunger made them weak; their four eyes seemed to gaze wearily. They licked the grime off his face, and Raphael fell asleep to the warmth and syncopated rhythm of their halting breath. Raphael woke up cold. Kaufman did not wake up, not at all. He died during the night. Let us say, in peace.

The embalmer added the Prince to Raphael's name and changed Kaufman's to Nimitz, God of the Odd—from the ancient land of Mesopotamia—and only asked for 50% of the gate. From the beginning, Kaufman had been the centerpiece of the family fortune. As Prince Raphael pushed him up and down the eastern seaboard, he would remove the sheet that covered the elaborately carved mahogany tank where Kaufman would float eternally for two cents a look. Raphael never tired of staring into the mismatched blue green glass eyes, more focused than true. The embalmer had provided them free of charge.

"Ladies and gentleman, step right up and witness the greatest curse that Satan flung down on we mere mortals." His English was that good, yet he couldn't quite comprehend the language when someone said, "You bunko-con, give me my money back. I wanted to see me a live animal." He learned that "fucking guinea wop" should have a sting. But that sting soon healed when two cents became two bits. Two bits turned to four bits. The pushcart acquired the donkey. More towns, shorter time.

He returned to New York and used the embalmer's

money for a dowry. Then he had a wife. His donkey became a horse. The country grew to the cities, which sired surrounding towns. Carts developed to cars; car to caravans. The caravan, which has now dwindled down to an old school bus, its banner of Prince Raphael, a pickled goat, and the remaining son of a son. Frankie doesn't look at the old photo in his glove compartment of a little boy sitting on his mother's lap and a broad-shouldered man standing by their side, edges frayed.

"Mother fucking glooming geek."

Fortunes change, and change again.

CHELSEA

"Take off your clothes," he said.

Chelsea removed her pink-checked dress, lifting it high over her head. She held it tight in front of her shivering body as she stood in the cold, damp basement with cement walls alive with green pus. She hated the Barkers' basement and all that happened here. She hated it when Barry first took her here and touched her in the "don't itch there, Chelsea," place and she touched Barry's "daddy's ding dong" part. She hated it when Ben promised to give her his new stuffed panda bear he got for his birthday but received a kiss instead.

She hoped she wouldn't have to touch Mr. Barker's "daddy's ding dong." Bart ripped the dress from her hand, leaving Chelsea in her slight cotton underwear. Her sleeveless undershirt had a little bow in the middle of the front collar. That's how she knew it was the front and why she was now allowed to dress herself if she didn't dawdle. Chelsea's underpants were decorated with faded ballerinas. Her skin was as white as her underwear, but contained no adornment or hidden instructions of any kind.

"The rest of it," Bart scoffed. "I need the underwear."

Chuck's youngest daughter wanted to cry, but was too scared and found no peace in any reassurance in the words, "Uncle Bart's not going to hurt you." She stepped out of the underpants and pulled the shirt over her head. When the undershirt came out from over her eyes, she saw Mr. Barker staring. Black eyes shined black, like the eyes of the mangy hamster in the pet shop driven mad by the constant tap tap tap tap tap tap tap tap tap tap tap on the window pain. "I'll need the shoes and socks."

Bart turned his attention to Lester and Lestim. Lestim was dressed. He wore Barry's shorts, but needed Ben's belt to keep them from falling off. Even though Lestim was as slight as Ben, Bart had dressed him in one of Barry's shirts, figuring the extra fabric that Barry needs, could be used to cover the cord of flesh that bind Lester and Lestim.

Bart took the towel from around Lester's shoulders. He knelt in front of her and ran the towel down her legs, rubbing gently, making sure she was dry behind her knees, around her ankles. He dried around the cord of flesh that joins them. Compared to the spiny arms and legs, this was their trunk.

Lester placed her hand on his shoulder to not lose her balance and fall over, taking Lestim with her, as Bart dried the bottom of her feet, his head bowed like a squire ready to be knighted. She stepped into ballerina underwear. Lester squawked, not quite a word, but a communication to her brother. Lestim replied, "Yes, he was happy too."

Bart already knew how he should slit the back of the panties to give room for their bond and then with a small safety pin, secure the top. He already had a plan in his head that he would do the opposite with the dress. He had made a bit of a mess out of Lestim's shorts, but Lester's dress remained intact: perfect. A little princess he would call her, if he was her father. Which he wasn't.

He took out his pocket comb and wiped it clean on the towel. He combed the tangles from her hair, careful not to pull. Her hair fell perfectly into a side part. Bart wondered why Betty hadn't borne him girls. He should have married Helen. She was good at girls. Gave Chuck two of them.

Chelsea sat on the floor. Her arms wrapped around her knees. There was nothing more than fifty cents of raw minerals contained in her whole transparent body. She shivered and bit her lip. Bart couldn't understand her frightened look.

"We're done."

Chelsea ran up the storm cellar steps and across the yard, not yelling till she reached her property.

The twin's old clothing sat in the corner. He burned them, but kept the note he found: Here are Lester and Lestim. Lester is the girl. Lestim is the boy. They will answer to neither/nor. Bart had written on the back, a dozen eggs, a loaf of bread, a gallon of milk. All the things he was to buy on his way home from the office. If he had gone that day. If he had ever gone again.

"What happened to your clothes, dear? How could you lose your clothes?"

Chelsea cried and was rushed up to bed with a fever.

The doctor gave her medicine, and she watched a lot of television for the next three school days and halfway into the weekend. Her next game of doctor would be played with a psychiatrist.

No one knows what happened to Chelsea's clothes, but the mystery of what happened to some silly little girl's clothing was quickly overshadowed by the disappearance of Bart Barker.

Betty cried a lot and Barry was properly spoiled by the neighborhood women. Ben was given what was left of the last cookie. Even Older Miz Schmitt was nice to the boys and brought them some of her special tea that helped them sleep and gave them sweet dreams. Chuck spent all the free time he had stapling up missing persons posters and trying to get a regional newspaper interested. Bart's disappearance was chalked up to debt, despair, and desertion. The newspaper space was given to, "Did you see that new kid in high school? He could really throw that football."

On Sunday Chelsea put on her blue dress and accompanied her parents as she always did. Betty sat next to her father, holding the hand of her oldest and dearest friend. Chuck had never had any boys. Barry looked uncomfortable wearing his twice-a-year suit for a third time. Ben looked small wearing Barry's last year's suit. He smiled at Older Miz Schmitt who nodded off before the Pastor called for a special prayer for the lost and their safe return. Chelsea flipped through her hymn book, not knowing what to find.

BART

Sure, Bart liked to drink, but he didn't drink to forget. If he left behind forgotten memories, his wind-up heart would stop and all that would be left was click, click, click of chattering teeth.

Or maybe he did—maybe Bart's consciousness (?) was so big it covered everything, so couldn't be seen, but he couldn't forget, so he wanted all to remember. Some walk on coals, sleep on barbed wire. Then there was Bart, carrying Lester and Lestim cross county. His barking like a sutra said loud, so all the Gods could hear and shout back, "I wrote that!" All beings are equal under the canvas tent where businessmen ran into governors, who ran into lawyers, children, accountants, secretaries, teachers.

Those who thought him a circus stooge bowed under his power. There were two classes according to Bart. Those who came and saw, and those who stayed home watching television. There was one class according to Bart.

Lester and Lestim—miracle of birth, vision of nature betrayed, reminder of the anger of God. Their naïve dance echoed their biological roots. Through a microscope, they looked the same: gene by gene, cell by cell. We could be the same. You be me. Now go back to your own body. The blood dripping down the childrens' chins, and spotting their previously stained, navy blue sailor suit could make a person hug their own child more than once a day for reasons beyond obeying the command of a bumper sticker or a celebrity P.S.A.

Bart at the table. Bart at the bar. Buy him a drink, which cost more than a ticket just to ask, "How do you do it, man?" The answer, so close to the eyes it crossed them. The question could only be answered in twos.

geek (noun) Someone who bites off the head of a live chicken.

to geek (verb) To bite off the head of live chickens.

Lester and Lestim, the least geeks. What would they do for a price that they wouldn't do for free and fun? To the vegetarian, a butcher was evil. To a Christian Scientist, the surgeon was perverse. The older gentleman did not understand the young. Lester and Lestim bit the heads off live chickens. A chicken was not a dog. A chicken was not a cat. We didn't even know why they crossed the road or how that could be considered a joke, much less the joke found in Eden were there were no jokes till the adorning of the fig leaf. What happened to the joke? The joke was lost. The light from the outside sincerity falls on the smile returned with smile - dagger. A slow poison - chronic headaches - stiff joints - wealth coma. Add it up - divide by two, plus or minus.

The joke contains no laughter. Death, the drummer's rim shot. Time to laugh, laugh, laugh.

Scrub the blood from the stage, from the corner of

children's mouths. The little girl with the tight perm says, "Yuck!" at the sight of all blood but her own.

Twitch, twitch—after the show is over, the audience gone. The premiere attractions, twins by destiny. Twitch, twitch, neglected to be informed of their impending death, the chickens' legs forget to die; remember to struggle. Bart shuts the lights. Twitch—in the dark, ignored ghosts haunt themselves. Who will steal the chickens tonight? Who will fry them tomorrow?

Tonight, Bart needed to talk. "I do it for the money, man. How about another round and some of those buffalo wings?" That was all he ever needed to say.

ROBERT

Robert sat in the back of the pick-up playing grandpa's old harmonica. Gazing up at the twinkling stars, he thought about his college entrance essay. "Tell us about yourself?" How could he fit his hopes, dreams, and aspirations into a one-page, double-spaced essay and still have room to add the clear, crisp night air?

Diane sat in the front and listened to Grandpa talk about the conflict in Korea and how he never trusted Nixon, no, not with his checkered past. Diane smiled at Robert through the window. He returned an understanding wink.

They had been looking forward to their winter break. That new town was getting claustrophobic. They were happy for their father's promotion and transfer and would never think of complaining, but if anyone had asked them, they never would have left Valhalla, N.J. They spoke among themselves, sometimes with anger, other times with pity. These people always seemed to stare at them. Were their lives so empty?

They were glad to get away from Bart and his group with their petty jealousies and fragile egos. Bart had, in his own way, invited them along on his Dionysian retreat. Robert had declined the offer for both of them. He wasn't going to let his sister spend a week with that group. He called his grandparents and asked for refuge without saying why. Grandma and Pops were wise enough not to ask questions, and there was no reason why Diane would ever have to know.

In town he could protect Diane, but at the campgrounds that Bart liked to go with his friends for drinking and fucking and shooting guns, it made Robert nervous.

As they drove up the winding country road, Robert imagined he was already enveloped in the smells of Grandma's kitchen, up half the night and all day cooking their favorite foods.

He already felt the release of swinging his backpack off and throwing it on the bed in a room that was exactly how he had left it: the calico quilt, the M.V.P. plaque from Little League. Though fond memories, they were of the past. Picking up another tune on the harmonica, he looked into the night sky. He thought of girls with perfect breasts and perfect teeth, like his sister's. He saw the big dipper, Orion, and Diane. There was music, too.

Diane had a harsh snap in her voice in reaction to Grandpa's laughter when she said, "His foreign policy was brilliant."

Grandpa beamed at her youthful exuberance and feminine anger. Diane's eyes burned up his hairy nose.

A hungry deer wandered from the depths of the woods in search of something fresh and green to eat. Instead, he was met by the high beams of the Ford pick-up. Grandpa's body stiffened as he swung the wheel right. Diane never saw the deer, since her head went first crashing into the passenger window before snapping back then forward, breaking through the restraints and seat belts and shattering the safety glass of the windshield.

Robert was lifted from the bed of the truck. The harmonica flew from his hands. He felt no sense of doom, but a floating. To be so young and have reached something so near perfection—why shouldn't he fly like a god? Not having been handed an orthodox upbringing or any curiosity for spirituality, he didn't know what to call his feelings. When his spine hit the tree and his head a rock, he knew the word he was looking for was "pain."

BART

Bart sat at the counter and ordered a glass of milk. It came with ice. Milk wasn't something he thought needed to be ordered straight up or on the rocks. He swirled the glass looking for an olive.

What was the dry-cleaning slip in his pocket for? That wasn't why he went into his breast pocket to begin with. He was looking for something. Something he had lost that wasn't his nipple. This was to be the first move in retracing his steps till he was distracted by the old receipt. He remembered the name of the town printed on the slip, but never knew the name of the establishment itself. It wasn't more than a location in a block on a street that ran through the middle of a town, a location that he would find again next year to reclaim his cleaned tie.

They will look in the back of the shop and probably not find it. Blame will be thrown. Voices raised. He will stomp out in anger, sending shudders up a woman's spine who crosses his path as she enters with her husband's suit, five cotton shirts, and a casual sweater for herself, rushed to the dry cleaner after a coffee caprice.

Bart put the slip in his wallet between his Social Security card and driver's license. He tried to remember what the tie looked like. Stripes; a deduction, not a memory. Though a paisley pattern that decorates the back of playing cards is not out of the question.

YOUNG BART

"No fucking way, I'm saving for a car."

"Bart, I can't tell my parents." Nancy who would someday change her name to Betty, dried her own tears.

"Anyway, how do I know it's mine?" Bart smirked, having practiced that line over and over and now completing his grand performance. Nancy didn't shout "encore" as he walked away, leaving her to carry her own social studies book. Bart checked his penis to confirm it was still attached. He walked into biology class and punched Scott Larson on the arm because he could. He took his seat in the back row, opened his book, and adjusted his attitude.

When Ol' Mrs. Schmitt walked in, Bart didn't notice the usual sallowness of her cheeks flushed, or how her hands trembled as she fiddled with last week's test, as she looked for the proper words to say.

Bart caught Chuck's eye and pumped his hand, hidden behind the desk. Chuck responded with an obscene gesture of his own. These guys could communicate.

Ol' Mrs. Schmitt's voice wavered as she said, "The principal has a somber message for you. We met on this subject this morning and feel you, as young adults, have the right to know." The green box that contained the civil defense speaker, popped before the thin voice of the principal came through. Dust driven free from the vibrations, slid down the chalkboard racing to be the first dust to the floor.

"It is with deep regret that I inform you that during the holiday week pzthzch an accident rmnphrn. They are both now sphlmw. The family will be zkmplt Rtpzch after school to Qurmld. Let us all blmct for them."

Ol' Mrs. Schmitt would always remember the day that somehow, with the help of God, she had maintained her composure. The students were in shock. How was it possible? It couldn't be! This was the best they could do? A radio you can hold in your pocket sounds a million times better than what they'd just heard. A low roar swept across the room. Each student looking for a word, a phrase that might have helped them decipher the message. They converged on the auditorium after school, where maybe the voices would carry and they would finally find out what was so damn important.

The assembly was the largest ever. The principal spoke rather clearly, a member of the E.M.S. had an urgent message on the importance of first aid, and even Mr. Richmond was able to leave the hospital for a moment, where his two children lay crippled and maimed, to say a few words of gratitude.

Later, in the darkened waiting room, Mr. and Mrs. Richmond hugged each other as if it might be their last time. Tomorrow, Mr. Richmond would bury his father.

BEN

Ben came to when the Moon was in the sky. He was surrounded by a blanket of warmth. Breath warmed his ears and ankles. A long, long tongue stripped his chest while little teeth nibbled the hairs on the back of his neck. Ben tried to keep his eyes closed. The feeling was good. The reality would be more than a little boy could stand. If this was one of God's tricks, the feeling of love, the vision and smell of hell. Ben thought little boys need not pray.

When a wet nose rubbed against his cheek, the reflexes in Ben's eyelids slid open and stuck. He stared into a large black eye on a small head with a pointed snout and fur. Ben wanted to scream, but was only able to create a rumbling from his chest. A cub barked. No, that was Ben.

The cubs felt sorry for the hairless creatures. He seemed so fragile and ugly, besides, Ben's ugliness made them nervous, but mother knew all about babies with fur or without. No one ever told her when to feed her babies or to clean them or to give them warmth. She even knew how to care for grotesque children like this one.

Mother's hot breath melted the blue tip of Ben's nose. He was about to feel it again, and it hurt. The tears that fell from his eyes were quickly wiped away.

The brothers and sister dallied around Ben playing their games. Coaxing Ben to join in. Weak from cold and hunger, he nestled next to Mother. He found a nipple and suckled from the wolf.

GREGORY SIMON

One day after school, Gregory Simon was putting a penny on the railroad track so the 3:46 freight would flatten it flatter than a flapjack. Then Gregory Simon would have a flattened penny, which was worth more than one cent. He was hoping to exchange it for a cigarette the very next day at school; that being the going barter price.

He was running late. The 3:46 freight was down the line. The horn blared once, twice, thrice. Gregory thought, "Uh-oh, I'm running late for the 3:46 freight." He put his penny on the track and ran to hide in the bushes, which is what you did if a penny was invested on the track; watch the penny and the train and anticipate the 'morrow when the flat penny would be welcomed into your peer group with a minimum exclamation of, "Wow."

He tripped and fell. The whole town agreed it was a tragedy. Some people thought the Simons were luckier than Betty Barker, who, since her husband's and son's disappearance, had changed back to her maiden name of Nancy. At least the Simons had a body to bury, if not enough to view.

At school, the name Benjamin surfaced. Barry used his brother's ghost to scare the big kids away. Since his brother and father's disappearance, Barry had been beaten on a fairly regular schedule. Fairly regularly meant every day, excluding a day for rest, Sunday not always being the sabbath.

There was an assembly at school. The principal introduced the chief of police, who introduced a real railroad engineer, who spoke about the dangers of playing on the tracks. They asked for questions. Is there life after death? Did it hurt? Did the train flatten the penny too? There were no questions.

YOUNG BART

Bart, out of cigarettes and already feeling the effects of a hangover that in all fairness should be reserved for morning, stuck his hands deep in his army surplus jacket as he made his way up his street. At three thirty in the morning, on deserted streets, in a sleepy, stifling suburb, there was nothing to do, with no one around to intimidate but the squirrels, and even they were asleep in the tops of the trees. "Fucking Rats," he said and kicked an acorn into the storm drain. He thought how hard-pressed he'd be to find fucking rats on this side of town. Morning dew slapped the night air. Bart wished he had a button left on his coat.

He heard before he saw the Richmonds' Urban/Rural Roadmaster. It was followed by a rented ambulette. They turned into a side street that was now called, "Where The Richmond's Live," rather than its previous name Jefferson Road, after our third president and author of the Declaration of Independence. Bart took chase. He stopped and hid opposite the Richmonds' house on Richmond Road, behind one of those lovely maples that are found in the older, cared-for neighborhoods whose money comes from the same stock as the trees.

Robert was already being lowered on an elevator platform from the bed of the ambulette. His head lay to one side and his wrists twisted in. He fidgeted for something to grasp onto. Mrs. Richmond cried, "He should have worn a hat!" She had forgotten how cold it could get this time of night. The elevator hummed its way back up.

"Please Mom, I want to stay! I want to stay with Robert."

Bart ran across the street to peer into the ambulette with room for one more.

Mr. Richmond held his wife's hand, "It's best for her, dear. It will be alright. They'll take care ..."

Who was that small body with disheveled hair covering its face? A face so horrible it seemed formed of melted wax. The platform swung up like a forbidding prison wall. "I want to go home," she screeched like the eagle who, having lost its way in the fog, lay broken at the foot of a cliff. Bart whispered, "Diane," as the ambulette door closed and drove away. Tears tumbled from his eyes, chin, cheek in the steady rhythm of an I.V. drip. The parents stood arm and arm. Her mother couldn't help but to wave. Mrs. Richmond, this is not the morning bus on its way to school. You are sending your daughter away. Two children would be too much to care for. It would kill you. Yes, you're a mother but you're also a wife, Mrs. Richmond. Yes, Mr. Richmond, you're a father and you are also a man. This mile in their footsteps wasn't in their poly-filled gortex after-ski booties. Robert was totally helpless. At least Diane could cry. Robert gurgled: his contorted hand grabbed the lever on the wheelchair and rammed it into a tree, a lovely old maple.

"I'll get that for you, son." Mr. Richmond pried his hand open. They dragged the wheelchair up the three steps of the front stoop. Tomorrow the contractors would start on a redwood ramp that the Richmonds' would always consider an added-value feature to their fine home in a well-kept neighborhood.

Bart ran to Chuck's to awaken him, tell him what he's seen. Once said, it could be believed. Robert was a fucking idiot drone and Diane looked like some sci-fi monster. Sharp lines across her face, and she's missing an eyelid and a nostril. Diane, Diane, Diane; yet to share a dance.

He stood at the base of the window, knowing it was only a little leap to reach the first strong branch of the tree. Then to climb up to Chuck's window would be easy. He'd done it millions of times. Drunker than this, more tired than this, but tonight only Bart would know the secret. Tomorrow Robert would be in town, but tonight Bart had a secret he alone shared with Diane.

Bart went next door and jimmied open Ol' Miz Schmitt's screen door. He broke in and took her kitchen radio. She had to learn these weren't the good old days.

Robert sat on the stage of the school auditorium swinging his head side to side in a seemingly bad Ray Charles impersonation. His mother stood behind him, his father center stage, thanking all for their concern and support and knowing, that now that Robert was back, that they, the student body, would do everything in their power to make him feel at home. They also appreciated all the flowers, but Diane's funeral was small and private. You can understand the grief, I'm sure. Yes, the students nodded. Grief, something you felt for a hamster, goldfish, or grandparent.

The crowd was the largest gathered for a school event. Volunteers sat on their windbreakers three-deep in the front of the auditorium. Chairs were being shared in the back, squeezed in cheek to cheek. The entire A.V. squad had their faces pressed against the plexiglass of the light booth. Robert let out a shrill call to answer the rousing round of applause. They would have paid to see this. Yes, Bart nodded yes. He understood it all, though he had neither a hamster nor goldfish.

THE GANG

There is a winter camp in Florida for the circus children and their attendants, plus other occupations which are left idle during the cooler season. One Winter, following a prosperous Summer, Lester and Lestim went along for the ride and stayed in the one place, rather than tour the less than fulfilling winter southern route, which is what Bart would usually do, since he seemingly knew no other way to spend their Winter/Summer that maintained his solitude.

Towards the end of that time and place, after a mile of lanyards and enough boxes made of popsicle sticks to bury the dead, the time had come for the children to pay back by entertaining the grownups with their last-ditch effort at a friendly, healthy competition of a three-legged race. Lester and Lestim came in first place: number one, numero uno, we are the champions.

The parents of the second-place loser were pissed. They were the lion tamer, the most heralded and prestigious of all jobs, skills, arts of the parents of the offspring who spent their Winter/Summer in shorts and mittens; the sons and daughters of doctors, lawyers, and Indian chiefs being in short supply and at school. Besides, they owned the place, since they had the land; lions being in such short supply and a deceased father-in-law

94

previously of Ajax Auto Salvage & Tow, who had left his only daughter with a tidy parcel of land and cash and his only son with a drinking problem and a uniquely effective way of spitting the word "bastard."

The lion tamer and his wife, the former Miss Ajax Auto Salvage & Tow, bought and paid for the ribbons that hung around Lester and Lestim's necks; they owned the lanyard, and the popsicle-stick boxes to bury the dead in. Their own little son Gabriel liked the anger that his parents felt on his behalf; it was a touching way of saying "I love you" without ever having to address him personally or touch him in any way what soever. Poor little Gabriel with the perfect winter camp record, and why shouldn't he be the strongest, bravest, coming from the strongest and bravest much like the lions they trained to ROAR? The third-place winner was Sam, the son of the man in charge of the softball toss. Though not the most prestigious, he was the richest, next to Bart, though don't tell the lion tamer or any son of a lion tamer. Sam understood Lester and Lestim's first place win. One against two, when the one is also a two—it causes confusion, makes the head spin, and at times, makes no sense at all. Their win was fair and justified to him. Though more just, if those were his odds. He'd bet a slug on that or five dollars and a new pair of sneakers.

Gordon the Great confronted Bart with his problem. Loudly, in front of everyone, during a quiet dinner in the commons when usually all that can be heard is the rubbing of food against teeth. Bart said, "Fuck off," and spit out a cold pea he found in the mashed potatoes, not liking his fruits and vegetables mixed. The lion tamer, getting no satisfaction from his confrontation with Bart, kicked the dirt and beat his wife. An animal would fight back. Gabriel spent the night with his grandma; she looked great in sequins, considering her age and the teeth marks in her arm that have all but faded over the years. What a story she could tell about a half-starved cub that was like her own child. "That was long ago, dear. I've all but forgotten," is what she would say to herself when she woke up screaming.

A ringmaster cannot live with such rift in his midst. Much like Solomon, Frankie was leading his tribe with wisdom and ancestral laws through forty-eight of the fifty United States during a period of a nine-month year. His intelligence stretched in all directions, cutting him in two.

Seeing the once contented lion tamer burst at the seams, much like granny's jumpsuit, there were many who saw an opportunity for fun. Winter can be a bore when pretending to be a summer.

A petition was signed as a mockery of justice. If Lester and Lestim are two people, wasn't it a tie, or who touched first? Wouldn't there be a first and second? Then isn't Gabriel third? Third place: the shame, the shock, the disgrace. The whip had an angry timbre to it. Only the lions snored.

Sam would lose his third place. He didn't mind. Sons of sharks aren't supposed to get glory. He would go to the beach and rub the feet of the old women who wintered along the beaches of the peninsula state. He didn't need a medal for that, a quarter would do. Anyway, he would lie and say he came in first: the champion, number one, numero uno. Those quarters could buy him a nicer medal or a watch to tell him the time, the date, and the phases of the Moon. Who would he be hurting if he told this one lie, and what are the phases of the Moon?

Sam met a young girl who cleaned the bungalows where they were staying. Every day Sally would race over after school and change in the broom closet from her jeans to that pink uniform with the Peter Pan collar. They had fallen in love, her with Sam, Sam with her, with or without the Peter Pan.

On the beach they met a nice man with a diamond ring and hairy shoulders. He liked them both. They liked to be liked as much as they liked their Sam-loves-Sally, Sally-loves-Sam love.

He bought them nice clothing and Sam raised his foot rubbing price. His tan got deeper and his girlfriend called him sexy. The man agreed. One day the man brought them to his house. They wondered why he'd go to the smelly old beach when he had a beautiful pool waiting for him at home.

They didn't expect to need their bathing suits, so they hadn't brought them along. What a shame, it was such a nice day. The man said he was tired and needed a nap. "You kids make yourself at home." He kept the company of a Haig Pinch bottle and a pair of binoculars. They went skinny dipping in the beautiful full pool. It was clean. The smell of chlorine made them feel safe.

Sam watched Sally's tits get sun burnt. The cabana was so much nicer compared to those at the beach. They wrapped themselves in terry cloth robes, then unwrapped themselves again so they'd be comfortable in the Florida room overlooking the pool as they played with the remote control for the TV and each other. They hadn't seen any of the movies the nice man owned and wished they could figure out how to turn that on too. That's when they saw Horace. Horace was a great Dane who'd been sleeping noiselessly in the corner, but had decided to wake now and investigate these two nice young people. Horace laid his heavy head on Sam's lap. Horace was a good dog. Sally stroked behind his ears. Horace liked the way she smelled, once he got past the chlorine. Horace was use to chlorine. He could get past it.

The nice man came down the stairs naked, waving a gun. His Speedos had given him severe tan lines. They were not sexy, thought Sally and Sam. Horace was used to the nice man's tan lines. Having no opinion either way, he went into the back yard to chase a frog. He would catch it and hold it in his mouth till a big yawn would furnish the amphibian with a means of escape.

The nice man always had difficulty making decisions, so he could not decide whom to fuck first. So, he decided, first, he should watch.

They were both very young and just this side of puberty. The performance was uninspired. The nice man yawned. The frog escaped. Maybe there was an alligator in the channel. Maybe not.

The nice man used the barrel of the gun to break open Sam's anus. That was enough to make Sally wet, with tears. The gun's sight scratched. Sally didn't yawn. Neither did the nice man. Neither did Sam. Gabriel would not have cried. He comes from a background of dignity and assholes. Sam had no such problem. He let out a howl that made Horace think of his dearly departed mother and the Volvo that was her demise: license number 2XJ 331. He had never given that information to anyone. Instead, he waited patiently for evolution to take him to the point of putting pen to paper. He wept only when he thought of the final page that would be printed before the words "theend." Horace waited for evolution to bring him to the point where aptitude allowed for space between words.

Sam thought of his blood and the comfortable feet of the old ladies. A lizard crawled up the curtain. Sam lay on the floor. The nice man got a drink and Sally hugged a pillow. Horace raised his leg and pissed on an orange tree. Everyone is busy here.

Gordon cracked his whip. A lion roared gladly. Gwendolyn wondered whether to feed the lions their supper or to discreetly dispose of the red, runny meat and let Gordon work it out with a hungry lion while she dined on steak. Maybe even gain a few pounds in the process. What the hell. If father was alive.

The white rug ran red along the path Sam crawled.

Sally watched the fan spinning on the ceiling. The man's head was askew against the arm of the chair. Her neck was twisted and the gun rested against her temple. The nice man had trouble maintaining his erection. He cursed himself for his drinking but thought, "The sun will come out tomorrow."

Lester and Lestim fingered the shared medal that hung around Lestim's neck.

Sam made his way to his knees. The nice man thought about his first wife, his accountant, and his parole officer; he came. Sam slammed him on the head. Slam the man, Sam. Slam Sam Slam. Sally let out a cry as meek as the one coming from the nice, nearly dead man as he rolled off her and onto the floor. Sally and Sam took a shower together. They were young and in love. Some things do not change.

They let Horace in the house. He had caught a lizard. He dropped it at their feet and entered the kitchen to lap some water. The lizard dashed up the window sash and said, "Whew!" Sally and Sam had lunch while the blood drained from the nice man's body. The phone rang. They didn't answer. The machine did. The caller did not leave a message after the beep.

Frankie studied the shaky video made by the man without legs, who had to stand on his fingertips and poke his lens blindly though the crowd that was brought to their feet for the stunning conclusion of the race—once on their feet, an ovation easily followed. Searching one frame at a time, Frankie could clearly see Lestim touched the finish line first. Lestim should have the first-place medal. Lester the second, and the third…. Striped of his second place, on an endless tumble to third, Gabriel. He cried as if he'd just been sodomized by God, Mr. Rogers, or the Nice Man. He and Sam never spoke. They should have.

Frankie retired into his Odditorium and dusted the tank where Kaufman floated. He thought he saw a wink. Frankie breathed heavy onto the glass tank, then cleared the fog with the sleeve of his worn sweater. He asked, "Is that an approval of my judgement? Was that which I saw pride?" The clear mis-matched eyes would neither confirm nor deny.

Sally took the gun that lay next to her head and put five bullet holes into the back of the nice man in a random pattern. Sam took the gun from her and placed it on the back of the nice man's skull. There were no more bullets in the gun after Sam fired. The Nice Man (Nice Man is capitalized because it's his name) never kept an extra bullet in the chamber, for safety reasons. Having a gun in one's home does have inherent risks; there can be an accident, a loved one could be shot, it might be stolen and find its way on to the streets where random firing can kill the most innocent of children asleep in a stroller. Therefore, there was not an extra bullet in the chamber, so only 6 slugs found their way into the nice man's body. His blood soaked the carpet, tearing at the Scotch Guard protectant and finding its way into the deepest of fibers. No one was ever going to get that rug clean again, no matter how hard they tried. The stain began to set.

Sam's father found the medal in a cigar box where Sam hides his most private personal possessions. Looking though the box he got very reminiscent, and there might have been a tear in his eye, if anyone had been there to notice. He thought of this box that once held shiny pebbles and rabbits' feet that now contained a pack of cigarettes, phony ID, and a couple of condoms. Sam's father removed the medal and thought he would leave ten dollars to say, "I love you." It was a nice thought, but the money was comfortable where it sat, so why break such a cozy relationship between money, wallet, and pocket?

The crowd cheered as the medals were placed around Lester and Lestim's neck. They danced in circles. The lions paced back and forth, avoiding the lion tamer, now mad. They did not know the difference between first and second and third. They did not even know the difference between freedom and captivity; then they would have known what winning and losing really means. They knew fear and hunger. They knew everything they needed to know.

Lester and Lestim sat at Frankie's table for a victory dessert of Jell-o and marshmallows. Bart sat to the side and smoked a cigarette. He thought the aerialist might be playing footsies, or it could be one of her leg cramps she gets. Gabriel was hungry. He would eat no dinner. He kicked at the lion cub who nicked his ankle. They had been more than friends. They were supposed to become more then brothers. With a kick and a nick, trust and fellowship flew away. They would never now be a source of a partnership that would provide for a future livelihood for both. The cub could go to the zoo and Gabriel to a technical institute. They'd called him Gabe. "Yea, right, man, you were a lion tamer and I was Cleopatra, now what about checking the oil?" The cub had no appetite.

Lester laughed so hard at a funny clown that a baby marshmallow flew from her nose.

Frankie moved in on the Bearded Lady. Her inner thigh was as comfortable as a mohair sofa, though it caused less of an allergic reaction.

Blood + Dirt = Mud.

Gabriel couldn't tell his parents his mistake was foolish. Only that he lost his only friend—for life—the cub, who licked his belly and went to sleep with the promise never to listen to that human cub with the pointy boots; He was a bad boy. He went to sleep without his appetite.

Sally and Sam had a sandwich and a tall glass of milk. Horace rested his head on the table and licked his face clear up to his eye. Sam thought that was amazing. Sally too. Then she began to Sally-sob a bit. That made Horace uncomfortable. Sadness made him sad. He had seen more than his fair share. Horace was a good dog. He went to the other room and took a bite out of the nice man's arm and licked the blood from his hairy back. It tickled Horace's tongue. He laughed on the inside.

Sam found his favorite music in the nice man's collection. He played it. Great sound! Sally went to explore the house. Sam got a carving knife from the kitchen.

Horace sat by Sam's side. It was good to have a dog by your side. Sam now had a woman, dog, and a corpse. Besides that, he didn't have a care in the world. He cut the nice man up and threw it in the plastic trash can. "Great sound!" he thought as his favorite C.D. played again. This time with a little more bass. Horace felt the music in his bones. It tickled.

Sally found the usual bedroom items. Pajamas, underwear, marital aids, but she also found other things she had never seen, not even in her parents' trailer. Cash, cocaine, and lots of rings and chains that would look great next to Sam's tan. The phone rang. The machine answered. Beep.

There was no joy in the lion tamer's trailer. Gabriel hid his ankle, which had begun to turn blue, and Gwendolyn was looking a might bit pink. The pancake make-up hid her black-and-blue. She had trouble serving the dinner because of the soreness in her arms. Gordon knew how not to hurt his lion, too much. Grandma brought over a cake, which only she ate. The seams of her pant suit shrieked, "No more cake, Grandma." Their tension was fueled by the laughter of clowns.

Sam and Sally hated to leave so comfortable a house, but it was time to move on. They packed Horace and the trash can into the Jaguar and hit the road. The nice man owned no Rand McNally and they could barely drive the car, much less figure out a GPS. They followed the sun around the world once every 24 hours. They drove to the next town and the town after that.

Sally looked nice in the fishnets she had found among the man's belongings. Though they bagged around the ankles, and Sam looked great in the open silk shirt, though it drooped at the shoulders. Sally loved the nice man's pigskin luggage. They packed what they could and put it in the back, along with Horace. He stuck his head out the window, took in the view, and sucked in the air.

The remainder of Lester and Lestim's camp time was uneventful. They made a lanyard for Bart's keys and a special little box out of popsicle sticks in which Bart put the lanyard before throwing them both out. They tried to learn a sing-around-the-campfire song, but there were words, and words meant language. Language, they did not need that. They tried to hum along, but there was a tune and there were notes and they had no need to hit them. They danced in the talent show. The applause was minimal. Their audience was other professionals, not a paying crowd stirred up by Bart. They never went horseback riding, and when they went in a rowboat, they never got offshore. Sam's father ran the softball toss by himself like he did before Sam was born, and Sally's picture found itself in the windows of caring merchants in town and stapled on telephone poles. She was a missing child.

BEN

Ben had always found his father's hands ugly, more animal than human; thick, black hair, coarse and ridiculously long, growing out of the knuckles of his fingers. Like burnt twigs they stood, two to four in a bunch, curled together in self-defense. It disgusted and embarrassed Ben that his father did nothing about it. Couldn't he have cut the hairs or softened or changed them somehow? He would shudder to think of his father's hairy hands running down the slender arm of his mother.

But now he looked at his hands. His brothers and sister would stare with him because they shared everything. He would stare and try to guess out of which pore would the first hair appear. How many would grow on what finger? How long would it take? One night he awakened with a start. The dream was on him, having his mother's smooth hands and not his fathers' pelt, but soon his fears were gone. His first hair appeared and it wasn't on his hand.

BART

"... these descendants of Adam." Bart saw his blue eyes. His sandy hair had turned grey, but he still had that baby face, that baby face that couldn't get him past a blind bouncer. It was Chuck, standing amid the crowd who now began to transform themselves from a chaotic mass to an organized system of matter. They stood in line. They waited their turn. They gave Bart their money, for they didn't know how else to retrieve their souls in a no-deposit, no-return universe.

Chuck and Bart had history.

They had history, like an earthquake, as a scratch. A breath, creating a rupture, pumping the heart through everyday words. They had history, Bart and Chuck. History, that blistered the skin in all the places colored by scars and sores and darkened birth marks in the shape of countries that no longer appear on any globe.

History as a corn, burnt and scraped from a foot that is forced into a pair of shoes again. Always to return. In the environment of the shoes, the shoes are thrown out and a new sensible comfortable pair is exchanged for the excruciating ones. The comfort is enjoyed till forgotten. The mirror hates the new pair. You have the mirror to thank for hating the shoes. A new, new pair beckons from the store window. "You love me. I am who you want to be. Put me on your feet. Put me on your feet." The corn returns, like the memories of childhood, post-diaper wetness never dries, never changes, it rests from time to time to achieve higher heights from which to fall. Legacy of embarrassment on the shoulders of subsequent generations bearing weight beyond their years. Sensitivity a form used in the performance to create perceived depth. Doesn't their memory hold the same picture? A victim hanging in a museum, run by on the way to the souvenir stand; expensive gifts for forgotten birthdays that lie between the diaper years.

Chuck and Bart were friends.

Chuck stood back, holding the hand of a small, dark-haired boy with one prominent eyebrow that grew from ear to ear. Bart took his patrons' cash slowly as he tried to figure where he might have seen this boy before, and didn't Chuck only have girls? He remembered one of them. No, there were two, two girls. Once they laughed. He thought he remembered that.

Dude spoke and broke his concentration, "What's a matter with you, Mister? Afraid to let us in? Don't want to sell us no ticket? Our money to good for you?" Those were the questions. No, Yes, No, were the answers.

"Yea!" the crowd agreed and pushed forward, throwing their money at Bart in the spirit of community giving. How do you like them apples? And Bart likes apples, a lot.

Chuck and Bart nodded their heads in acknowledge-ment. Their pupils shifted from side to side, neither finding peace in the other's image. Chuck took his young son's hand and walked to the softball toss. He won a pink elephant, which was carelessly left in the ice cream shop they stopped into on the way home for a promised treat. They returned to the store to retrieve the prize, but the elephant was gone. The boy's deep, dark eyes became clouds of tears. He would remember this day.

BART

Bart had an abscess on his neck. It was nothing at first, just a middle-aged zit caused by some misbegotten, unforgiving, reprehensible ingrown hair. He nicked the pimple while shaving, and it did bleed so he'd worn the tiny bit of toilet tissue on the wound. It read like a stop sign. He did not like the message.

So, Bart grew a beard; it had distinguished hints of grey. Some thought it gave him a bit of class and élan. Bart knew it did. He narrowed his lapels and procured a black turtleneck, which he wore on his days off. The random grey hairs sung praises to his maturity. The scab heeled and fell off, as all scabs do, while the hair, a lone hair, a solitary hair, the kind of hair that drops out of school, hitchhikes to Hollywood or New York and teaches itself acoustic guitar, grew deeper, tangling though the veins and corpuscles, not knowing day from night. The abscess bloomed like a Fuller dome, containing but a small portion of Bart's bile and pus.

Bart gave himself the night off as a consolation prize for his zit. At the bowling alley he met a nice young lady. She turned in her apron and joined him at his booth in the cocktail lounge. She ordered something sweet to drink with a slice of orange. He had something dry with an olive. She wanted his life story. He told her one. She listened while staring at his proto-Hemingway beard and gazed into his eyes that wore sincerity like disposable contact lenses. His pimple pulsed. She moistened her lips.

"Don't you bowl?" she asked in a whisper.

Bart said something about a bad back, and she offered to take care of it. The crowd in the cocktail bar followed their footprints as they disappeared into the sand. Eight pins down on the first ball with a difficult split ahead. The assembly laughed and hoped she had a condom. They knew he didn't. All laughed but one.

That man ordered a drink for the road. Took it in a paper cup. He drove home. He went to sleep. He dreamt. He is running. Running from a wall of water that chases him around the world; never-ending sprint as the tide brings the one ocean on a circular tour of our flat, barren planet. A woman sits high atop a mountain. The only rise of land on the globe. She calls to the dreamer. "Climb up here to me. You'll be safe. You'll be safe with me." As he stumbles up the mountain, the ground crumbles beneath him. That's when he realizes it is a mountain made of bones.

When he woke in the morning, he forgot what prompted him to say, "I never dream."

Bart's back was feeling a lot better. "Thank you very much. You should be a nurse." No, she just saw herself as a public servant. He kissed her on the neck and felt relieved that his tax money wasn't being wasted.

LESTER AND LESTIM

The bathroom in the service station is a safe place for Lester and Lestim; not being fit for either or all genders, it is fit for them. They like to look at the words on the wall, though they don't know how to read. They look at the words like pictures. They like pictures. They like the pictures on arms, legs, the chest. They especially like pictures on the back, it being a canvas they lack. They like the pictures and the words too.

Bart has only a small picture on his arm, but some people have many pictures. Lester likes to touch them, the pictures. The pictures lie flat, but the hair tickles her fingertips. The men laugh and burp; this is a first for them. "Look at the retard!" they might scream, none of the crowd with an awakened consciousness towards special ed. or challenged youngsters. Hell, they woke up and went to jobs they hated. You want to talk challenge? I'll talk challenge. Where's my fucking pity?

Lester puts her hands on his waist as they take off for a little ride on a motorcycle. Lestim waves good-bye to the world behind him and burns his leg on the tail pipe.

If he only knew how Lester peed and was able to comprehend the complexity and power of the neighboring muscles. He'd pull off the road and give Lestim a beer and Quaalude and do a little scientific research for the goodness of humanity. My goodness.

Over the years, Lester and Lestim have developed a need to spend a little time apart; adolescence is a time for isolation and self-reflection, then turns into the adult years, which is a time to discontinue the self-reflection as the isolation is brought to a crescendo.

Lester and Lestim did not have a normal childhood, though they did work out some stretch exercises, which helped separate them two inches. One day, overdoing it, they pulled a muscle and became closer than they ever were.

SAM AND SALLY

Sam lay face down on the motel bed. His fever was rising and falling like the full Moon, in keeping with his watch. Sally would run back and forth, changing the compresses that cooled the back of his neck and infected anus. They had traded the nice man's pinky ring to a doctor who gave them antibiotics in return. There was nothing for Sally to do but wait for Sam's screams to stop and fever to break.

Horace closed his eyes while licking the last of the nice man off his chops. Sally stroked his dinosaur-shaped head and kissed him behind the ear. There are now three mouths to feed. Still, she was glad for Horace's company. She envied his ignorance and enjoyed the little walks they took twice a day behind the motel. She felt safe with him even when the crazy people yelled at her from behind the chain link fence adorned with razor wire that all but circled the motor court, which had become her small family's home.

When Sam first fell sick, they had taken up in this motel. Sally thought she should be neighborly to the woman with mousey brown hair streaked with grey who would stand in her nightgown, grasp the fence, and call, "Psst, girl. Girl! Do you have a cigarette? They don't give me no cigarettes. Do you have one? Huh? Huh!"

Nervous and thrilled by the prospect of doing a good deed, Sally brought a pack of Winston's that very next day. She found the woman calling to hidden faces behind closed shades registered under imaginary names. "Do you have a cigarette? Does anybody have a cigarette? I want a cigarette!" Only Sally emerged from the motel.

"Here you are, ma'am."

The woman met Sally's eyes with pale spheres that didn't focus. "I hope you're not a menthol smoker," Sally said, trying to sound knowing. She held out the pack. The woman's slippers dug a little deeper into the dirt as she held close her robe and mumbled. "Do you have a cigarette? Does anybody have a cigarette? I want a cigarette!"

"Here you go. They're Winston's." Sally tried to stop her arm from trembling as she reached through the fence. "I have matches, too." Horace growled. The woman backed up, "Cigarette, cigarette, cigarette."

"Bad dog! Bad! He's just a sweet little puppy. He only looks mean." The cellophane crimped as Sally crushed it through the chain link. The woman moved inches closer to the fence but turned her body to the side. Sally saw that, since it was her good deed, she should do the work.

"I'm not going to hurt you." Sally took the pack and slid it just so much farther. "It's just you asked for cigarette ..." The old woman sprang like a lizard, grabbing the pack and two of Sally's fingers. Sally tried to pull away, but the woman would not let go. "You bitch! Fucking cunt!" The woman spat each word into

Sally's face, those and many more she could not hear over the barking of Horace. Jumping on the fence, his great frame caused the barricade to give, yet, not wanting to hurt Sally, he didn't dare harm the woman. Horace is a good dog.

Sam wished Sally would return. The hour had changed since she had gone for her walk and he needed her to switch stations from the hour of cartoons to an hour of cartoons on another channel. It was that time of day for him. They had gotten a deal by taking a room without a remote, so he was totally dependent on her. Sam swore to himself that it would never happen again. From now on he would have all control devices.

Meanwhile, Sally's pain was so bad from the feeling that her fingers were about to be permanently amputated by the grossly unhygienic method of having them yanked from her hand. She didn't notice two large men running up, being trailed by a nurse pushing an empty wheelchair. "Cock sucking, little whore," was the last thing Sally heard before "THUD!" That was the sound of the woman. Not the woman's voice, but the sound that her head makes and possibly many other heads when hit with a heavy blunt instrument that renders one incapacitated. She was rendered incapacitated.

The nurse called Sally a stupid little girl as she helped the orderlies push their docile victim over the neglected lawn. Horace licked Sally's face and cried for her. Then he remembered the reason for these twice-daily walks and found an interesting odor on an old rag. He lifted his right hind leg. Sally looked away. A pack of Winston's lay torn, the tobacco strewn from the paper that was its original wrap.

There was another woman beyond the fence. She was sitting in a canvas lounge chair, under an old oak. It had no leaves. It gave no shade.

She wore a large, straw hat that shielded her eyes. Her back was to the fence. A sharp reflection from the mirror she gazed in hurt Sally, made her close her eyes and look away. That was the first she noticed the woman with the mirror.

Horace buried the old rag. Saved for another day.

BEN

Ben hid amidst the newly planted public project evergreen trees and bushes on the island that ran between the north bound and south bound lanes of the darkened, deserted interstate. From across this thoroughfare, he spotted a raccoon's mask as it rinsed frayed beef from a discarded French dip sandwich into an oily roadside puddle. A raccoon always washes his food. Good for the raccoon.

The old lunch held no interest to Ben. The raccoon did. He was hungry. Hunting on this island was scarce. He could manage a few squirrels that had been stranded but had not had time to breed; boy meets girl, and that's it. Ben might also find a stray possum or mole whose hunger had blinded them to fear the car. They would dash to and fro across the road, following their noses in the dead of the night in search for where their next meal would be found. The ones who didn't make it to the other side would leave Ben to sniff around their legacy of rancid meat à la roadkill. Ben liked his meat fresh; killed by his own hands. It seemed to be good manners, and you never know when a guest was to drop by.

It has been so many years since someone had done a kill for him, and that had been his mother. One day she stopped. Ben was confused and kind of hurt. He went hungry the first day and the second day too, but a child will not starve itself. Mother had learned that lesson the hard way. She would always love her oldest cub Shallow Tooth as if he were also her youngest.

From then on, Ben has provided his own food. First, he was only able to catch bugs and small rodents. Once he got hungrier, he made his way to be a self-assured hunter of squirrels, raccoons, dogs, and cats.

When he was still in the pack, together with his brothers and sisters, they hunted down a regal buck. He led the kill, though it was his brother, One With Spot On Nose, who initially found the prey. As the wolves and Ben surrounded the animal, the buck clopped his stony hoofs. Thrashing his head, he highlighted his fierce horns, so cruel, so sharp, so mean. Bravado was no match for the six kin that embraced the buck with their teeth and claws. One With Spot On Nose leaped into the air. His teeth grabbed into the buck's neck. The buck jerked his head and shrieked with pain. The brother was shaken free, not without a mouth full of blood and skin. His own flesh wound didn't prevent him from charging again with reinforcement, those wolf kin who had suckled next to him.

Ben grabbed the buck's back right leg, felling the buck to the ground. His teeth sank into muscle, only to be stopped by bone. They ripped the hide off the buck as it finished its struggle: full defeat, full surrender. The wolf clan howled into the night sky. Howled at the grand buck's death. Howled at the joy in the sound of each other's howls. Ben stood up on his hind legs. Howling at life and death and all that was yet to be known. He waved down the Moon and licked it behind its ears.

And he stood; for the first time, he stood. At five foot ten, he felt huge in comparison to most of the forest's fare, but embarrassed next to the size and strength of the trees. His front legs were skinnier than his hind ones, though they were no thinner than those of his brothers and sisters, even One With Spot On Nose. His fur hadn't grown in, but his mother told him he always was an ugly child, but she loved him just the same. Though his teeth were blunt, he had the most remarkable front paws that could be made to move separately and elegantly, like a caterpillar, a bird, or a wildflower whose leaves dance by his side. In front of his kin, he would hold his fingers tight together, almost as a fist, as a paw. Ben doesn't do that anymore. Not since the night of the grand buck's death.

His siblings had heard about hunters: their tree-trunk legs, worm-like paws, and bright, blunt smiles. What they heard had scared them. Instinct said flee. Love left meat on the grand buck's bone. That was the last time Ben hunted in a pack.

The red Mustang convertible barreled down the darkened deserted interstate. As the driver hit the brakes, a quart bottle of Miller and its friends Walker and Daniels slid out from under the front seat, then rolled back into the covert place keeping in time to the girl in the passenger's seat, whose head kept the beat with a fierce bump against the windshield. She held her forehead and said, "Ouch." Her lip bled. She had bit it. "Ouch," again she said. "What did you do that for?" She snarled at the driver and turned the rearview mirror to face her. She sucked on her lower lip. "Ah, shit."

"Thought I saw a wolf." The driver held his wrist. It would be a long time before he got his backhand back. "Ah, shit," she said again.

"Are you alright?" His concern was a martini. Tonight, in the role of sincerity, Vermouth.

"How am I going to explain this?" She touched her lip gently. How quickly the purple bruise spread around her mouth.

"You might need a stitch." He reached between her legs and grabbed his friend Jack.

"I'm not going to some sped out emergency room quack." The taste of blood and the piece of lip she has still not found in her back teeth held no special interest to her. She grabbed a bottle. Johnny kissed her mouth. It hit her lip like death. Johnny Walker made her cry. The alcohol killed the germs that could have led to a nasty infection sometime in the future but not tonight.

He saw her tears and handed her his handkerchief. He loved her. He loved his car. He would miss his handkerchief. He loved his handkerchief. He handed her his handkerchief and started on down the highway. They passed no other vehicle till they got to the state road. Not worth a name, just a number from 1 to 10. No one passed this way for another quarter hour. By then, Ben had ceased his cries and crawled his way towards the old "all but abandoned" road, into the underbrush of an open lot that lay between the muffler shop and the new Seventh Day Adventist Church.

Ben looked at his naked body. Looked closely at his wounds. He had seen this type of flesh and blood before; in his kills, in the other animals that he had pounced on, torn at, ripped his teeth into, never on his own self. It brought back a loving memory of his sister, One White Paw, how they used to play on a similar roadside, how they would chase the squirrels and chipmunks, not only when they were hungry, but sometime just for the fun of it. Mother didn't like that. "It's a waste of energy, and it could be dangerous besides," she would growl.

They would bow their heads, lick their crotch, and say, "Yes, Mom." Then they would return to play, to rub on the grass, nibble at each other's ears.

That's when One White Paw saw it, the reflective eyes of a feral cat as it stalked a field mouse on the other side of the way. Ben wanted to play and scratch and lick. One White Paw saw the green eyes and tasted the thin strips of white meat that she would find running down the back of the cat. Each of the back muscular legs would be another mouthful for Ben's small, sensitive sister. And the brain is for licking. "Big kill, little kill, the brain is for licking." That's what they sang when they laughed and played and nibbled on each other's ears.

She bounced off the fender of the car, but not far enough to bring her home safely. They kept coming and coming, the cars. Ben's little-boy howls weren't louder than the horns that kept the cars from swerving out of their lane. By the time Ben reached her, nothing was left, even for a remembrance. There was no last whimper, last kiss. No time to nuzzle with unspoken love and regrets.

Since then, Ben had been careful with the roads and the cars. But tonight, as he looked away from his raw, bleeding leg, he longed for a wet nose, a rough tongue, someone to say goodbye to. A beetle crawled past his nose. He ate it, then passed out.

His blood soaked into the ground where the big top would stand the day after tomorrow.

FRANKIE

Fucking this. Fucking that. Fucking the other. Frankie cursed. If the word was God, Frankie was a pious man. Bart stood leaning in defiant casualness, bathing in the wrath of profanities that was occurring for maybe some little box-office indiscretion, a ticket glitch, or sophomoric antic. He felt as if he had swallowed the head of a chicken and it was still snapping at the lining of his stomach. He didn't like it. How do Lester and Lestim do it? He would give them a raise if they had a salary.

The canary caged in the corner had a different perspective of the scene. She always had the view of Frankie's bald spot. Friar Frankie, she would tease if she could, but she couldn't, having been a bird of the "pet stop and shop" variety that didn't have more than a 2nd grade education.

As Frankie's temper crescendoed, she would notice, with fear, the veins that pulsed and pumped in his skull. The extreme use of vocal cords would tighten the muscles in his neck, letting the blood pump up, but not fall. He would get redder and redder and his head bigger and bigger till a map of the Mississippi delta would show itself in full glory to the little bird. She could spell Mississippi and Oklahoma. Meanwhile....

Bart might have been concentrating on the veins in

his forehead or neck, or on the weather and its relationship to space and time, and how none of that had any bearing on his gas mileage.

The canary knew about the veins on Frankie's head. She knew she was a sitting duck—sitting (D.U.C.K.) in the cage watching Frankie's head redden as the rest of his body went white and clammy. Clammy, she could only surmise, being born with a desire for seed not shellfish.

One day Frankie's head exploded. The police came to investigate. They took many pictures. No one noticed the weak chirpings of the injured canary. Bone shrapnel struck her wing. Blood dusted her feathers. She lay weakly on yesterday's sports section and today's shit. No one noticed. But....

Lester and Lestim heard the anguished chirp. They crossed the police line and entered the trailer through a trapdoor. They knew where the injured bird lay. They took the injured bird from its cage and ran it home in a flurry of giggles and one or two twitters.

Borrowing Bart's tweezers, they removed the shrapnel and cleaned and bandaged the wound as they had seen Bart clean many of their own scrapes and bruises. The canary, having first assumed the worst, felt reprieved. The kids were getting older, and no one ever mistook a canary for a chicken. They made a little bed out of a shoe box and tucked her in. Nighty night, they all squawked. Comfy and cozy, she relaxed.

While waiting for sleep, the canary heard Lester and Lestim debate on what to call her. Lester liked the name

Bird. Lestim wanted to call her Dog. Since they were both adamant, nothing was going to be settled that night. They decided to sleep on it. The canary dreamed of a name with a sort of a continental flavor to it, like Camille or Ingrid.

A couple hours later, Lester and Lestim woke up and bit the head off the bird. She was never to receive a name.

THE WOMAN WITH THE MIRROR

"Oh, girl, so you're back again."

"I have to walk the dog," Sally said, stepping away from the fence as Horace began to growl. Sally wrapped the leash around her hand and held on firmly, knowing that if Horace did decide to attack, the only thing accomplished by this act would be a sure dislocation of her right shoulder.

The woman with the mirror turned her back on the scared, young girl and agitated pup. She tossed her head to the side, twirling the straggles of hair through the air till they fell limply below her shoulders, "You do not see I am the most beautiful woman in the world." She pitied the young girl's ignorance as she gazed deep into her reflection. The mirror caught the sunlight and rested it in Sally's eyes.

"I'm sorry ma'am. I can't see."

Horace sat down on his haunches and rested his large, wet nose in the sand.

"I can't see."

BEN

A big plaid man with a large red mustache nudged Ben's battered body with his steel-toed boot, "Wake up, man."

"AAGGAH!" As Ben tried to turn, he realized an appropriate howl to match his pain. It was "AAGGAH!"

"What the hell happened to you?"

Ben's mouth was so dry that, though he needed to shout again, he could not. "Aaggah." He opened his eyes. Through the rays of the sun, he saw one that resembled him more than One With Spot On Nose. Ben whimpered from his throat knowing this man, One With Red Drooping Lip, would understand. "AAGGAH," he tried to say, but could not.

"You're fucked up.," One With Red Dropping Lip said. "We've got to get you to the hospital." Ben wondered why this ugly one wasn't licking his wounds as the pack would do. The wonder caused fatigue. Fatigue drew his eyes to a close. When his eyes were closed, the sound of Red Drooping Lip's voice became hollow. Then the voices in his own head started to sing, "Sunny day, sweeping the clouds away. On my way to where the air is sweet. Can you tell me how to get, how to get to Sesame Street?" His brain rolled from consciousness to ... the letter "Z."

Ben woke in ten minutes when the siren attacked the

field, leaving a tire track so worth the effort of making a plaster mold and hanging it in some yet-to-be-built museum. It should have cost a cry, a sigh, a shout, an "aaggah" when the perfection was destroyed by some trotting sneaker with a worn sole. The ambulance landed at Ben's side. One With Red Dropping Lip twirled the tip of his mustache and said, "Get him the fuck out of here. I got people coming."

The saliva found its way back into Ben's mouth in the form of a thick raging foam. He yip, yip, yipped with no yipiyiyo yiyea attached.

Aaggah! Aaggah! AAGGAH! Ben got very loud as they strapped him onto the rigid, narrow board, raising his cry from small to capital letters. They clasped a collar around his neck. This was his first.

His howl sent shivers down Lester and Lestim's spine as Bart drove onto the campgrounds.

"What the hell is this about?" Bart asked One With Red Drooping Lip, who Bart called Red, which was short for Jim, that came from James; the name of an older brother to his father who had drowned in a lake on a beautiful summer day when father was too small to remember either the boy or the grief that followed, but would hear the stories of how everyone loved him. That's what they said. He was something special. They tell him that too. As the baby brother who was to become a father got older, he remembered how he heard them say how young the good die. Still, he named his son James, which became Jim, then changed to Red, and will be known to one as One With Red Dropping Lip, and though he's in this story, it's hardly worth the mention.

"Hey Red, what the hell's going on?"

"Some guy, really fucked-up. Not a stitch on."

"Let me know when you find her." Bart and Red exchanged laughter over the thought of a naked bleeding girl that would be needed to make a matching set. Bart pulled away and into the most discreet area of the campground. He supervised the raising of his tent, met with the Chamber of Commerce, and granted an interview with the local weekly that, in all likelihood, would not make it into print till a week after they had gone, causing some dozen or so people who read the newspaper to show up at the vacant lot and say, "Damn, missed it." They would go home and finish rummaging through all the pages of the newspaper, whispering, "Damn, missed it again."

When the anesthesia wore off, Ben awoke in the hospital. He saw a wolf standing over him; Ugly, like he was. No, even uglier. He didn't think that possible. No fur, but the nasty stringy kind from her head, which didn't even cover her snout. The rest of her body, the part that wasn't masked by her white uniform, seemed to be as smooth as the rocks in a rushing stream where Ben used to sit with One White Paw on the hot summer days and watch as Ben's skin would transform into that of a goose without its feathers. The whole pack would gather and marvel. Even though Ben was ugly, he was loved.

They howled with awe as his skin turned blue in the snow-fed stream.

"How are we feeling, Mr. Doe?" she said with a blunt smile as she wrung out the compress and placed it once again on Ben's forehead. Ben felt a rumble in his guts from where his spleen once dwelled. It could almost be called a purr. This cross-species dialect would usually scare Ben, but today, it seemed no matter. "Purr." He inhaled deeply, trying to see if he had met this ugly one before. Not even One With Wet Nose, Floppy Ears, or She With Black Hind Leg was this appealing in odor, he thought as be began to sniff. Ben had only heard about She With Black Hind Leg. That's if you can believe everything Broken Fang had to say. And no one believes everything Broken Fang has to say. It's not that they wouldn't have liked to.

"You must be very thirsty." She held the plastic cup and its straw before him. Ben tried to reach his snout into the cup. Scoop the water up with his tongue, as he was accustomed to. Female ugly one pulled it away. "Mr. Doe, what are you doing?" The water spilled. She stared at the large water spot that covered the front of her dress.

"That's alright, Mr. Doe, accidents happen.," she said, catching hold of his confused indigo eyes. His wavy curls of steel black hair picked up highlights of blue from the Sun that snuck though the hospital blinds. "It will dry," she said as she became a goose without her feathers.

The nurse thought about what a joy it had been to

bathe him. More fun than a Crackerjack box or Tootsie Pop because each layer of blood, dirt, and disinfectant she removed brought its own special treat; another muscle defined, an artery teasing with a steady pulse. She wondered how she would bathe him now that he was conscious. Would she shy away from certain parts she has previously scrubbed squeaky clean? Would he shrink with embarrassment? Ben wonders if she'd turn blue for him.

"John," she whispered as she wiped the water from her clean white dress in long, casual strokes. Never has she seen a man so beautiful. Not in a spring water advertisment or daytime television. "John Doe."

As he laid in the hospital bed, fifty stitches in his side and his right knee held together by metal poles, a tray with Fentanyl, Vicodin, and Xanax by his side, "Oh, Johnny, Johnny, Johnny." Could this happen to a physical therapist? She thought not.

She would bathe him. She would nurse him. She would work doubles and on weekends by putting up a brave front saying she needed the money because she was thinking of going to med school or the Caribbean. Look how sorry he was that he spilled the water. She would forgive him now and over and over again.

Ben heaved himself up. Lurching for the water carafe.

"Mr. Doe, please be careful. You've been in a coma." I've been in a dream.

Ben stuck his snout deep into the sterile vessel and lapped up what he could with his long, hard tongue.

"You're an animal," she said in a growl. She poured the water into a metallic emesis basin to give Ben an easier time drinking. Specks of water flipped from his mouth hitting her like a birthday sparkler: her cheek, her neck, her lips. "A real animal."

She ran her hand through his mane. He rubbed his head along her forearm then grasped the limb securely between his teeth. She didn't pull away, not then or when his hardy tongue ran down the length of her face to where the button of her dress flashed. "Wait."

He sniffed at her skin through the layer of thin, damp cloth. Ben wasn't sure. Wasn't sure what he smelled. He buried his nose deep inside of her.

"Mr. Doe, someone will catch us." She pushed him away, checked the hallway. The coast is clear. The metal rings of the privacy screen scurried around the bed. The buttons on her dress flashed, "Wait no more."

As she lifted her dress, Ben found a place so warm, so familiar, so close to home. This wolf wasn't so ugly after all.

For a man without insurance, Ben got very good care.

THE SOLIDER

The man in the maroon Chevy followed the carnival for five days before being discovered. No one bothered to question him. Questions asked, responsibility taken. Responsibility taken, liability incurred. There seemed to be an inordinate lack of curiosity, considering mankind was involved. Gossip created civilization. No pyramids of marble columns were to be left here.

He wore his hair close to his head but natty, like a newborn pup. His freckled yellow skin gave him a past. His grey eyes held no future. He kept his wheelchair in the back seat, along with his extra shirt and pants. He sat on a lambskin cushion that didn't stop the sores. During the Summer, he drove with a towel over his lap and nothing else. The peanut butter jar he peed in was the predominant smell, over and above the pine air fresheners that hung in a clump from his rear-view mirror, next to a red paper poppy and his purple heart. They stayed with him like brothers.

Sometimes he pulled off the highway and imagined the stars over him, beyond the light, beyond the clouds, beyond the roof of the car. He knew there was a God and still might be, if he only had a sunroof to confirm and verify.

The solider gave the fair young man in overalls and no

shirt four bits to dump and wash out his jar. He never saw the jar again. He spent the day cruising around for the boy. His throat was parched, but he dares not drink, his bladder deaf to the commands of his mind. His search crept into the dusk.

The empty field was stacked with carnival trailers. The fair young man was freshly washed, his hair parted on the side and glued to his forehead to keep it from falling into his eyes and blocking his view of the lights and sounds, and pretty girls. His new dungarees were folded twice into neat cuffs. He was with the prettiest of the girls. And since she smiles her hellos and sways on the balls of her feet during goodbyes, she was the prettiest of the prettiest. Which was pretty, pretty.

Though he could have bought two cotton candies with the four bits—he liked cotton candy and could have eaten both—he bought only one. He shared that cotton candy with her. He hoped to find something sweeter and what could that be but a first kiss, quick and stolen under the shroud of a warm, pink sweet-spun sugar?

A thread of sugar hung from her mouth. He removed it with a peck of his lips. She blushed and looked down but did not say, "Oh, you're so gross." She tasted sweet, sweet, sweeter than any mother, sister, aunt he'd kissed before. His shoulders were strong, and he was glad he'd taken a splash of his brother's cologne. He'd thought he'd seem like a pansy; instead, he felt like a man. He never noticed the car lights behind him as they walked arm and arm towards the Ferris wheel. He prayed, knowing there was a God, "Let the Ferris wheel stop when we're on the top and let her be scared enough to hold me close, Amen."

"There is a time to forgive," thought the man in the maroon Chevy.

This isn't one of them.

A time to forget.

He can forgive his mother.

He can forgive his father.

The friend who said goodbye.

The ones who didn't.

The dog that died.

His country.

His God.

But there was no forgiving
the skinny kid who ran off with
his peanut butter jar.

The boy was killed instantly.

The girl lingered for two weeks.

He felt bad.

A man might do many things
and think a few things more,
but one thing's for sure,
a man has got to pee.

FRANKIE

"You little mother fucker. What the fuck do you think this is, little mother fucking sucking piece of shit?"

Frankie slapped Sam on the back and said, "How nice it is to see you again, you mother fucking sucking piece of shit." He welcomed him aboard, gave him a map to the next town, and told him his Dad was dead, deserted, or jailed, but wouldn't he be proud just the same. "Bart will be eating his own shit when he sees what you've got." They laughed in camaraderie. They laughed because the other one laughed first. They laughed because they had used up all their words and were tired and didn't really like each other. They laughed.

Sam and Sally and the most beautiful woman in the world had enough money for a room with a kitchenette or two singles. The most beautiful woman in the world said she could make homemade soup. Since neither Sally nor Sam knew what that was, they went for the kitchenette. They were looking forward to a new life, filled with riches and fresh new experiences. Tonight, they'd dine on soup, homemade.

After slurping a thin broth of carrots, turnips, and chicken necks, Sam and Sally tried to make love as the most beautiful woman in the world moaned in the bed next to them. Late at night, after Sam had fallen asleep from his pain pills, exhaustion, or boredom, Sally stayed awake and listened to the whispered tales of the most beautiful woman in the world. She told of a fairytale life of the beautiful young Diane, who managed puberty like an empress having her straight, brunette hair combed once for every slave she owned, the most popular girl in high school. There was her light, fair brother and the dangerous lover who was the spark and excitement. From one she had unconditional love; the other, unrequited desire. This virginal Diane could not be one in the schoolboy's harem. She wanted him alone. Him secretly. She had him that way alone in her heart. She said her dangerous lover must have felt it too. He must have known her unrequited pangs of passions and spent all his dreams on her as she did on him. The most beautiful woman in the world inhaled softly. The one eyelid she had fluttered.

"Where are they now?" Sally whispered carefully so not wake Sam, whose restless breathing caused little dots of perspiration to form on the back of her neck. "Did they ever do it?"

"No," the most beautiful woman in the world said huskily as she scuffled back to her twin bed in the double room, "They never did it."

Sally thought it a wonderful story, full of all the childhood she missed out on, but could not understand why they never fucked each other. That's what Sam and Sally did, and though they really, really loved each other, it was in no way a fairytale romance. The most beautiful woman in the world tells very old stories. It must have happened once upon a time, long, long ago. People are smarter now.

SALLY, SAM AND THE
MOST BEAUTIFUL WOMAN IN THE WORLD

Between driving the car and keeping the small-talk road conversation going for the week that they'd been on the road, Sally was exhausted. Sam and the woman with the mirror hadn't said more than a word to one another. Sally wasn't even sure if it was more than a grunt. Sam shifted uneasily, spinning the donut shaped pillow he sat upon. The woman with the mirror gazed at her reflection while running her fingers over her uneven brow. At least there was Horace, who unwittingly rescued Sally twice daily with his walks, which gave her a moment to breathe easily rather than remain squashed between their uneasy silence. Horace was such a good dog. Everyone said so.

When Sally saw the Ferris wheel off the road, she shouted, "Let's stop!" as she careened the car through three lanes of highway traffic. Sam agreed, saying, "I hate these things," hoping to find a fairly decent, out of the way port-a-Johnny where he could take his suppository. Sam was psyched about that.

Sally knew that at the end of the day when they were to be on their way again, with cotton candy in their veins and the spin of the Ferris wheel in their heads, Sam would sneer something like, "Hope you had fun," before he would inflate again his comfort pillow and ease down into the car. She would know he had a good time, but would love him even more for his sacrifice; being in a constantly miserable state must be tough for him, but it was his way of keeping her the happiest person in the Plymouth that pulled off the highway ramp and made a couple right turns past a gas station with convenience store, motel with cable, and fast-food restaurant with rest rooms for customers only. They made their way to the fair grounds.

Sally always considered these things fun, fond memories. For Sam, a carnival was a reminder of his childhood, a jaunt in a meat packing plant. But to make her happy....

"You stay here." He flung his words into the back seat. The woman with the mirror dimly nodded. "If that's alright with you?" Sally threw in as a courtesy. Sally liked courtesy. She liked the courtesy that Sam showed her. She didn't want the woman with the mirror to seem unwanted. Or, if not wanted, to know courtesy as Sally knew it.

"You children go play." She ricocheted these words off the looking glass.

Sam grabbed Sally's hand and she stumbled after him through the fairgrounds, leaving Horace in charge. He was such a good dog. Everyone said so.

The woman with the mirror hummed her tender song. Horace brought his heavy head to rest on her thigh. His soft brown eyes looked through her thick scars and then closed into a restful doze. Her voice rose and became like delicate ribbons behaving to the wishes of a benevolent snake charmer. These ribbons of lavender and gold teased the unsuspecting lovers, the friends, the tired worn-out families to come closer, to hear the voice, the words, the wisdom of the woman with the mirror. They slowly gathered around the car bathed in warm light. The dirt dried under their feet. Horace yawned lazily. He batted his long lashes.

They scratched their heads and wondered what they were doing here, standing around a beat-up car when the noise, excitement, fun, and fair was not one hundred yards away on the same undeveloped field called carnival grounds for three days only a year, or per annum.

They looked at the car as if it they were sixteen and this would be their first. They looked suspiciously at the car, as if they would be more embarrassed than annoyed if they drove it a hundred yards, only to have it die. Then a blind faith took them away. Car and spectator, the most beautiful woman in the world and Horace, became responsible for the feelings of the other. She opened the window. The crowd drew back in a gasp. The sunlight made the crisscross scar across her cheek glow. The pupil in the eye without the lid imploded in the light, leaving nothing but a milky sphere. From years of sitting in the beach chair at her resting place, her body had grown into a rectangle. Horace sniffed at her knee, knowing nothing about osteoplastic surgery.

She held up her mirror and told them she was

beautiful. And they believed. She spoke of her sensitive eyes and full lips. They hung their heads and agreed. How could it not be so when she said so? She talked and ribbons forbade them to move. Their acquiescence nourished. She spoke of cascading waves of hair, and even the man with the severest of buzz cuts could feel the wind turn into the hands of the most beautiful woman in the world. Run her fingers through his locks. Her words became riverbeds of hidden treasures, smooth, shiny pebbles and freshwater lakes forever renewed by primordial springs.

As she talked, her mouth became dry. A cherub in a plaid jumper and sneakers lifted to the most beautiful woman in the world her lemonade glass. She sipped and the crowd sighed at the coolness, at the tartness, of the liquid that quenched the thirst of the most beautiful woman in the world.

"What the shit is this?" Sam saw the crowd around his not-so-legally-owned car. He was torn by the moment. Should he turn around and slap Sally for getting him involved with that ugly bitch, or should he make his hand into a fist and deliver it directly to the party responsible?

"Don't be mad," Sally shouted after him, as he marched through the mud, fists clenched. His few gold plate chains clanging together, keeping up with his Sousa steps.

The most beautiful woman in the world took a deep breath and closed her eyes. A cloud traveled over the Sun and rested in its warmth till a breeze shuffled it along to merge with friends as they gathered to rain.

"Get the fuck away from my car." He pushed his way through the dissipating bliss.

Sam jumped onto the hood of the Plymouth. His thick-heeled shoes dented his hood and woke Horace up with a start. Horace's tongue hung hungrily, and breaths came in quick succession, followed by dribbles of spittle that tended to create respectable puddles on the backseat floor mats.

The crowd, exhausted but pleased, turned to leave. Sam saw something in the crowd, something he hadn't seen since he was a child, attaching lead slugs to the bottom of Coke bottles for his father's soft ball toss. He had snuck away one slow night when his father would have had the time to drink his gin and beat his son. He had snuck into the pit show, the top show, the ultimate in his world. He had snuck though the canvas of Bart's tent. He didn't watch Lester and Lestim bite the heads off of chickens or dance their stupid dance. He had seen that before so many times that it was as commonplace as a pop fly in softball or the open fly of his drunken old man. He snuck though the canvas and stared at the crowd. He couldn't call them happy as in Christmas day, or happy as he felt when he was inside Sally, but they were happy, nevertheless. And felt more so when they paid Bart the extra dollar to see them drink the blood from the chickens they beheaded. They paid for their happiness. They were squared. They owed nothing to man nor God and most of all they were squared with Bart. "You're looking the wrong way, boy." Bart spit the nub of his toothpick at Sam's feet. Sam ran from the tent and took a smile with him. It wasn't that he was happy, as in Christmas day, but happy because he was smart now. Learned something. Something good. Something his father couldn't teach him. Because his father didn't know. He ran back to the soft ball toss and stacked the bottles into pyramids in a way that the eye could not help but see a win, but the laws of physics would just laugh at the futile attempts of the locals' fast balls.

Sam looked into the eyes of the congregation gathered around the Plymouth and raised his arms as he would imagine a preacher doing. He raised his arms and thrust out his chest in a way that expended more energy than Moses needed to part the Red Sea. "My dear friends and family, you have witnessed here today for the first time the most beautiful woman in the world." Now it was time for the world to square it with Sam.

The most beautiful woman in the world opened her eyes and bowed her head. Horace wrapped himself in a circle on the floor as best as he could. He knew this wasn't his show, and he modestly stepped aside. Horace was a good dog. Everyone said so. The discarded popcorn bag Sam passed through the crowd became heavy with coins. Sally was brought to tears, not only filled with pride at Sam's spontaneous oratory, but that she was not alone in seeing the most beautiful woman in the world. She jumped into the Plymouth and wrapped her arms around her. "I love you very much," she said and the most beautiful woman in the world agreed and how Horace was a good dog. Sam counted the change and let it rest heavy in his pocket. It felt rich. He had himself his own pit show.

"What the fucking shit is this fucking shit?" A little man with a red face bolted across the parking lot. Frankie hadn't changed a bit. Sam had.

BEN

"We'll miss you, Mr. Doe," the nurse said as she pushed his wheelchair out the front door.

"Thank you," Ben was able to mutter, after his brief hospital stay. Ben had relearned his "pleases" and "thank-yous" by hearing his kindly nurse, the female ugly one, repeat those pleasantries time and time again.

No, she wouldn't give him her phone number or offer up her apartment and her willingness to support him the rest of her life. "Thank you," he said as he stood on his shaky hind legs. His nose met the air, uncaptured air that flitted around outside. He found an unsure direction to start in.

She wanted to whisper, "We'll always have ICU," but prudently thought it better to begin forgetting. "Good luck, Mr. Doe." She could stop working doubles now.

"Thank you," he barked.

SALLY

It was late at night when Sally went trudging back to the most beautiful woman in the world's performance tent. She was looking for Sam. Her head jutted forward; her right arm swung tyrannically forward and back, forward and back. She held her left hand in front of her nose to hide a shocking red blister of a pimple. The mound of the pimple seemed like a volcanic island in the placid south seas, dripping in its own angry shit. The center of the maelstrom sent out a strong enough beacon to bring the Flying Dutchman safely to harbor or toss it into a final abyss.

The most beautiful woman in the world had already finished her bedtime snack, warm milk with honey and dry wheat toast. She was snugly in bed, asleep, breathing lightly through her nose. Her deviated septum made the walls of the trailer whisper. "Sweet dreams, sweet dreams, sweet dreams," she seemed to snore. Sally was sitting up alone getting bored, then worried, then lonely, then angry, then worried again. Sally marched back to the tent with strident strides. Her footsteps sunk deeper and deeper into the mud, saying, "I'm here. Now there. Not there. Now here."

Sam must know that she hated visiting the tent when the most beautiful woman in the world wasn't there. It was then that it all seemed so dirty and ugly and boring. It made her worried and angry and alone and worried. Sam must know how she felt about it. She must have told him a million times. She must have told him once. He must know. Why would she need to tell him?

Sam was in the tent with those spectators who were earlier basking silently in beauty, now cheering ravenously at a black and white Boston terrier and one dozen hungry rats as they instinctively tore at each other's flesh.

Bart was there too. His hand gripped tightly around a fistful of fives and tens. He smiled. It was weird. Sally never saw Bart in this tent before. Sally never saw Bart's teeth before. Sam complained that Bart never once went to his show. Most barkers try to check out the other shows, even if it's to steal bits of presentations or a few good barks strung together in the most desirous way. Never once had Bart set eyes on the most beautiful woman in the world. It was like Sam's show wasn't good enough. Anyone who entered the tent wearing a big hat or thick mustache or whose pupils nervously ticked from north to south or north to any other direction. Sam would say, "That's him. Bart was at the show today." It seemed that was all Sam ever talked about. That and the money he was making. Sam smiled too. She had seen his teeth. She had learned the difference between a grimace and smile. She did not keep score.

Between Bart and Sam, the two best damn barkers after the poets, prophets, and politicians, they could pry a man's pocket from a man's pocket. Teach him to gamble away everything down to his underwear or even the underwear, its value being greater when removed, so someday they could tell the story how they even lost their underwear one night, rat-baiting in a side show tent. "...wonder what ever happen to those people? Strange lot, that carnival crowd, but I'll be damned if they didn't run off with my underwear. Left me without a stitch. Made my way home in a cardboard box. That was a sight, I tell you. I was quite a sight wearing that cardboard box. Not a stitch on underneath, as the day I was born..."

Bart and Sam didn't care how a man told the story, as long as they were willing to bet their boxers on their learned scientific analysis prediction on who would win and who would die. It kept them from running if the cops raided, and it also invented a whole, new way of gesturing and talking. It gave Bart and Sam their own stories and another beer, this time on me.

There was one naked woman with large tits and a bigger laugh, known to the townsmen as "she's okay," so was tolerated in their fraternity. As she slapped the young ones' asses, Bart's curiosity about her faded. Their eyes caught for a minute, but recognized each other as familiar terrain. Bart desired the desperate "we're going to die at dawn" of those with the deep religious conviction of only the thoroughly fucked enter heaven.

Bart and Sam kept their clothes on. Why not? For Bart it would be redundant, since his body hair made him seem as if he was wearing a mohair suit, and Sam could never find a story to explain away the scars on his backside; not one of noble dignity, not one that didn't end with him crying his eyes out into the deep thick fibers of a Berber shag with an asshole, with a gun in his asshole.

No spectator complained about the garbed conductors, because who of them would dare show their all-in-a-ring of snapping hungry rats that Bart and Sam would coax on to snap at the needle-toothed Boston terrier? Sure, it was a small dog. A family dog, some might call him; good around kids, but a watchdog, too, not much trouble to groom, cheap to feed. It was a small town with small rats. If it was a city or rubbish oasis with mounds of piled trash out back of restaurants, three to a block, Bart and Sam would have picked themselves a pit bull or a Doberman, for argument's sake. People believed in pit bulls, believed their press and innuendo and respected those that were costumed in thick leather collars if they were neither skinny nor pale. But a small town, with less garbage; to Bart and Sam, the rats seemed nothing more than mice with a bad haircut.

To the Boston terrier, with his bulging eyes, running in circles with nowhere to retreat, slipping on his self-made rile as excessive saliva ran from his mouth. The dust, the dirt, the eau de cologne made breathing difficult through his squashed nose.... To the Boston terrier, this was not his definition of a good night.

Sally walked into the tent. The Boston terrier yipped

loudly as it shot one rat from its head, another rat snapping at its tail. There were two rats lying dead. One mangled beyond rodent recognition. The other lay quietly, peacefully, on its back. Its front paws look as if they are comfortably clutching bedclothes. Mouth, slightly ajar so it seems breath would make a contented whirl. Sally expected Mommy rat to say, "Billy, it's time for school," and to see Billy wake up, grab his lunch pail, and run off to catch the bus leaving his homework behind. "Oh, that Billy," Mama rat would say with a smile and a nod.

The Boston terrier let the rat in its mouth fly from the grip of its teeth. as another rat chewed on its back paw, while a third one managed to get into its kidney. To the Boston terrier, this was definitely not a good night.

When Sally saw the terrier's confused, frightened eyes, what she had been rehearsing as a calm request turned into an anxious plea. "Sam, aren't you coming to bed?" The cheering crowd called cease fire to all but the rats and terrier, who had crossed the line from performance to art for art's sake.

Shyly, Sally answered the silence. "It's very late and I thought I heard a noise."

There were plenty of volunteers from the crowd offering to see that Sally wasn't lonesome tonight. The woman with the big laugh egged on the bidding to show once again she was "okay."

Sally looked at Sam, waited for him to put up a boundary, but not with Bart there and the crowd wanting to learn more about Sally, how soft her hair was, how she smelled when she perspired, what her favorite color was, what was the precise strategic ploy that caused the downfall of the Spanish Armada. She hid behind her hand. Her pimple pulsed in its privacy. It was pink. The crowd circled around Sally. Their eyes had a need and hunger, which was just like what she might see in them when they stared at the most beautiful woman in the world had the fence been torn down.

The money in Bart's hand itched for the company of more. He wondered if the rats wondered how she might taste. Or, if Sally was a rat and Bart was a pit bull with cruel eyes and crueler teeth, if she would have the nerve to pounce on him before his attack. And how her head would feel in his mouth as he shook it from side to side to break her neck. Would she still struggle to survive, would she nip at his gums and tongue? Would Bart open his mouth, releasing the rat? Would Sally, critically injured, scurry away only to get done in later in the night by an undeserving cat? On meeting her Maker, would repair come under warranty or would cash be required? Would Bart's existence linger under the pall of plague caused by the bite of the feeble rat? Could Sally find a reasonable mortgage or a payday loan if she was a rat in need of repair?

The Boston terrier wailed. It attracted limited attention. Nevertheless, the show must go on. A canvas wall was torn in two. Bart was the first to run at an unexpected intrusion. Call it experience, practice, cowardice. Bart did not see the young hairy man with the indigo eyes howl and flay his strong arms. The spectators grabbed for their clothes, running into the arms of others reaching for their fig leaves. Quick, God is looking.

Sally stood, her arm fell to her side as she saw the young man dressed in denim take the rats in his hand and throw them away from the suffering dog. He looked like he could sell cigarettes, fragrance, or beer. But no; intent he was on becoming the terrier's hero. So much so that he didn't hear the screams of the spectators as a rat with nothing on its mind but to clench its sharp teeth would be thrown across the tent to land on their naked bodies. Sally didn't turn her head as a scream nearly deafened her right ear. She wasn't even aware that a man standing just so close had a rat dangling from his nose, eating its way up his face.

Sally might have hoped it was Sam who was running to her side to sweep her out of the tent, but after she saw Bart leave, she knew that Sam wouldn't be far behind. Probably already changing the story into myth and charging whatever is on tap and corn nuts for concession to a fable told.

The spectators ran home bleeding. This all happened in June. No children were born in the March of next year, and April only saw two births. The town council tested the water and shrugged their shoulders. The men traded their jockeys for boxers, and the woman with the big laugh let out nary a giggle. They were thinking they could close a school in five years' time, but by the time

154

July came around, they shelved the notion. The gene pool was back and running. Cats became very popular, and the chief of police became baffled when he couldn't discover who was killing anything small and furry, from field mouse to squirrel. He scratched his head and closed the case.

Ben bent down to one knee and picked up the dog. He breathed heavily into the pugged nose. The tent was empty but for Sally and her pimple, as quiet as a fresco on a church wall. Moving only enough to blend in with the breeze that finds the tear in the tent that Ben had made. The breeze manages to skim away the odors of the blood and screams and reveal the faint reminiscences of the most beautiful woman in the world. The tent looks so different now than in the afternoon when it was bathed in ribbons of lavender and gold.

Someday Sally would react in an emergency, run or stand and fight. Maybe utter something like "help," for example, or let loose with a long high-pitched shriek that would make dogs reply, "Huh?" and people bolt up from their easy chairs and ask, "What was that?" But tonight, she stood like a board and breathed as a board would breathe. Ben tried to lengthen the dogs squashed-in nose, hoping to give it a brave long stout like One White Paw. The frightened dog struggled in Ben's strong arms. He nipped at Ben, but bled his own blood. Ben took his skilled tongue and bathed the little Boston terrier's wounds. His saliva seemed to have a soothing quality. The terrier moaned before it died. Sally thought he heard it say, "God bless." Ben heard a distinct, "Woof."

Ben licked it gently, futilely, over and over. He had come to depend on his tongue for so many things that now he hoped it could be used to give life. Enough to see the terrier to the point of wakefulness. Then he would limp away to find its way home to a bed of dried lichens. His place to die. Ben nudged his muzzle with his nose and ran his chin around his ear.

Sally watched this strange man, so fierce yet gentle. She thought she heard a tear fall, but saw it was his sweat. Either would satisfy her. She didn't know if she should talk, clear her throat, say hello, or dismantle all her molecules and rearrange them outside the tent, disappear forever from this man's world.

Then, she started to breathe again. It was something she usually did with grace and ease. Tonight, it became kind of a pant. It caught the attention of the young man with the strong tongue and indigo eyes. He looked up, which was Ben's "go to" when he heard panting. He always hoped it would be One From Pack Of Many.

Ben saw her, the light young woman standing motionless, glistening in the stagnant tent. A beacon called him to his own late bed; as he laid with One White Paw, my love. Nothing could be done for the terrier. It had done its job. It was time to go. So long for now, Bowzer. Better luck next time.

Ben knew he would not die alone. Sally realized she

would not grow old with Sam as this strange, fierce, gentle, kind, mean, angry, man took her in his arms. Ben lifted her dress and pulled down her panties as he did with all the other hairless ugly ones. He was going home to where the animal was formed of soft stone. She reached for his genitals, the area that was so hard for him to stretch and lick, though licking there had always come easily to Three Grey Whiskers. His organ changed to something strong and proud. Sally held it assuredly and put it inside her. He knew it would be safe there, like a warm house on a crisp morning, coffee on the table, breakfast in the iron skillet. Time to get out of bed, lazybones. Ben moved about from room to room: the antique boxes and framed family portraits, a rack of world's greatest dad mugs disappeared from the walls and became the dark caves where howls echo and the bear sleeps to be awakened. A dozen wolves, like hungry rats, escape the starvation of a barren winter.

Bart looked into the tent and thought of a bucking young boy trying out his wingding on a girl named Nancy, who later changed it to Betty, who would bear the man two fine sons, but for now they fumbled in a gully between the football field and Mr. Parker's split level. Bart couldn't remember the book he read that story in, or if he'd ever read a book. He turned from the young couple, closing the canvas flaps of the tent behind him. There was something about that boy he liked. He didn't like that.

Bart walked up to Sam and threw his arm around his

back. There was nothing about this boy he liked. His arm landed like a club. "How about a drink, buddy?" Sam, he never liked. He liked that. Sam wanted to tell Sally he would be at Bart's for a drink, but Bart said, "What are you, pussy whipped? No way, man."

He had a drink with Bart. Bart kept him there for two drinks and three,

Sam talked loudly, bragging at what a man he was. All Bart could do is agree, knowing that his lady was fucking a mad man. He spit out a nub of his toothpick.

Sally's brain fought to hold on. She knew Sam was near and repeated to herself over and over again, "It's only a penis. It's only a penis." Yet she fell into her own vagina. Her skin on her back grew raw from rubbing against the dirt floor. She looked into the eyes of the man on top of her. His pupils were pitch and wide. Wide enough to see in the darkest night. To see into the corners where no one dusted. Into an area of Sally where the door was doubled locked but side window open. He climbed on through the window. Found the comfortable living room chair and gnawed the stuffing out of the upholstery.

She dripped around her head, drenching her hair, closing her eyes. The high functions of her brain flew away. Sam was less of a name, less of the memory, and she the most beautiful woman. Clumps of grey matter dripped from her thigh. Only the brain stem was left. But her vial organ kept working and working well. So did Ben's. The cave walls danced with crystals. Specks of gold clung to smooth stones that were drenched in waters that were not tossed out of heaven but freed from earth. The bear spewed his last word as he took a gulp of death's blood. The wolves howled. Ben the loudest.

Ben stared at his penis. So did Sally. It was really great, thought Sally. "Woof," thought Ben.

HORACE

Horace died. They found a chicken bone where he laid dead. Big dog felled by little bone, and he was a good dog, and he was a nice dog, and he was a sweet dog. It took two strong men to carry him to his grave. He would be missed. He was a good dog. Some whispered, just as well, a dog that size, that age, hips begin to give. Sure, he could chase a squirrel to the last of his days, but recently with a bit of a limp, though barely perceptible, a limp, nonetheless. How he loved to chase squirrels. Never caught one. Loved to chase them. They say he liked cheese. He was a good dog, a sweet dog. Everyone said so. He would be missed.

SARAH

Sarah was in the front row, holding her new little puppy. She really didn't want to be here, even though the carnival only came to town once a year and it was no less a day than her birthday—what a lucky girl.

What a wonderful present it should have been: Her whole family was there, not just the protons, electrons, and neutrons, but the noble gasses and radioactive elements as well. All there but her sister, who had run away. So highly flammable, she would have ruined everything. Yet, her absence made it a little hard to breathe. There would have been no one to leave Sarah and her new puppy home with. A puppy is not a sister. A puppy is not even on the chart.

Sarah was never alone. No, Sarah was never left alone. It would have been scary to be in a big house by herself, it was thought. With her new birthday puppy, maybe the house wouldn't have been so scary. At least not as scary as "this." She'd cried till her parents agreed to let her take her puppy along, held in her trembling arms. One day Sarah would teach him to fetch, give a paw, or play dead. "What do you want to be when you grow up?" Today he learned how to shake with fear. "I want to be a teacher."

When the show started, Bart asked all the children to

stand up close so they could see. Sarah's parents thought this was very considerate. Their little girl gave up all hope to rest her anxiety from behind her father's thigh. She clutched the puppy so tight it whimpered. Sarah couldn't hear it over her own sobs and the taped pre-show music Bart played to add a little professionalism to the act. The tall people parted for Sarah to make her way to the front of the line. It was her birthday, after all.

Lester and Lestim came on stage, not as the cute little children in the poster, with sailor suits and bows, but as those awful scary teenagers Sarah had seen outside the movie theater Friday night, or hanging out by the bike racks behind the library. It was what her sister had looked like before she left Sarah, her family, and home and the dog she never knew. Sarah had always crossed the street to avoid them. Her mother had told her to do so. Sarah thought all teenagers had something contagious. Which was why, even when her sister was home, she'd never leave her room. The first visible sign of the disease is blotchiness of the skin, leading to reddening of the eyes, poor posture, and slurred speech turning into satanic tongues. And there she was. Her parents had sent her up for a closer look at the Devil times two.

Lester and Lestim slumped across the stage, their tap shoes replaced with unlaced sneakers. Lestim had holes in his T-shirt and tears in his jeans. When Lester yanked at her shrinking halter top, her metal bracelets clattered to her elbows.

Sarah would swear (well, she wouldn't swear) she thought she heard them whisper "go to hell" or "fuck you" or something else deserving of a slap across the bottom. "Damn" raced through her head, though she wasn't sure what it meant: "Damn, damn, God-damn," as the music failed to provoke Lester and Lestim into their dance. As Lester and Lestim walked in their routine circle, a strange man patted little Sarah on the back and whispered, "Don't you wish you were a twin, little girl?" A salted drop of water caused a gully in the puppy's soft brown floppy ear. Lester and Lestim did their move where they try to walk in opposite directions but are pulled back. Ha ha; always elicits a response from the audience.

Then Bart picked two chickens from the cage, throwing them out onto the stage. No one had informed Sarah that the crux of the show was to watch someone bite the head off a chicken and drink the blood. Even when she overheard the word "geek," she was only expecting to see four-eyed Justin from her kindergarten class.

If anyone had bothered to ask Bart what went wrong with the show that day, he'd be hard pressed to tell them. Was five shows a day too much? Maybe they just weren't hungry, or on a diet maybe? Kids that age, we know how self-conscious they can get. No matter, Bart didn't know why, after Lester and Lestim bit the heads off the chickens, they took the carcasses under their arms, and squeezed the carcass in a combination bagpipe, water pistol move. The first three rows were thinly sprayed, without favor. It was a showstopper. Bart refunded the money and was out of town before the first laundry bill hit.

He could have beat those two, but they wouldn't have cared. Instead, he purchased 50 cent ponchos for the first three rows, and it was a two-buck bargain to be a V.I.P. under this canvas dominion they went on from town to town, five shows a day. Sometimes there was a christening, sometimes, there was a poncho stuffed with disappointment in a glove compartment. Damn, most would say, till a cloud burst and then thanks and damn rolled over in bed for a quickie.

Bart changed the newspaper that lined the bottom of the chicken cage. There in a picture on the front page was Sarah. Bart didn't see the photo, and if he did, he wouldn't remember the face, and if he had read the article, it might have been a bit like this, Young Sarah O'Conner was hit by a car running across the street trying to catch her dog. The driver of the maroon Chevy did not stop. What a shame, on her birthday, no less. The dog was still missing. Bart turned the paper over. There was a war somewhere.

The chicken in the cage was grateful that the show was down for two days of travel. Since life is short and she knew it, she did not dwell on the mishap of Sarah but ate her seed, took a drink, and tried to pluck out the eyes of a friend. It is all part of another day of life in a small cage.

BEN

Ben did not notice the most beautiful woman in the world was the most beautiful woman in the world because all the hairless ones looked the same to him. She turned her head away from this man who looked at her and not the reflection. She brushed a few wisps of hair with the silver-handled hairbrush Sam had let Sally buy for her at a garage sale a few towns backs. Sally whispered into her cauliflower ear, "I think we're in love." The most beautiful woman in the world blushed and let out a tear. She wanted to say, "So you think so." Or "Who do you think you are to find love?" or "Sam will be brokenhearted. How can you desert him after all he has suffered?" She wanted to do something to stripe the gleam of satisfaction off of both these young, thoroughly fucked people, but all she could do was let out a sound like a dying frog. "Croak," she said.

Sally embraced her bestest of friends. "I knew you'd be happy for me."

A deadly acid brewed inside the most beautiful woman in the world. When she started burping, Sally ran and brought her some medicine to comfort her pain. The most beautiful woman in the world needed more.

"That isn't a pimple you've got there, is it?" She

drank down her antacid and belched once beautifully. Sally's hand jumped to the front on her nose.

"I don't know where it came from."

"You sit here, I'll take care of it."

Sally sat at the boudoir as the most beautiful woman in the world mixed a drop of this, a splash of that; alchemist magic to turn lead into gold. Sally sat demurely facing her as the most beautiful woman in the world soaked a cotton ball and patted the inflamed area. Sally thought it smelled a lot like witch hazel, but was happy to be in someone's hands who cared.

Ben slipped out of the trailer and into the moonlight. He removed his penis from his pants to give it room to breathe. Lying on the dirt, he admired himself. His shadow fell to the ground. "Woof," thought Ben.

BART

Bart took the bacon from the pan and cracked the eggs open, dropping them into the sizzling grease. He felt he was getting old again as he adjusted the flame on the propane burner. If not old, at least redundant. There was a knock on the door. A tentative slight knock, more like the scraping of knuckles against the door than a knock, knock. "Who's there?" Bart hoped a splinter was involved in the confrontation. Ben was late. He knew the boy didn't have a watch, but he was late and now Bart was caught in the act of cooking his dinner. He didn't want to be watched cooking. It makes a man look unloved to cook for himself. Or at least alone, and maybe redundant.

Ben stood, with his hat in hand, though he didn't own one. The knock became a scratch and a whimper. A chip of red paint found a home under the fingernail of his index finger. Bart opened the trailer door. The smell of bacon slapped Ben across the face. He felt alive and close to death, like the time the ice gave way as he pawed for fish. The cold was as instantaneous as an animal's instinct to flee from danger. One with Grey Stripe pulled Ben from the icy waters. He shook for hours. Ben wondered if he'd shake later as he stung from the slap of bacon. He knew there would be no Grey Stripe today to pull him from his present icy terror and that he would not turn and run. Ben was born in the suburbs. He had instincts.

"They say you say you were raised by wolves."

Bart and Ben walked circles around the other, the greeting more animal than human. A sniff filled them with the information held in a scent that was organized and catalogued before being cross referenced in their libraries of familiar odors. Words appeared in the air, father, son, father, son. Neither dared read the bubbles that blossomed from their heads.

"Thank you."

"You expect me to believe that?" Bart removed the heating coil from his coffee mug. He added a heaping teaspoon of instant coffee, a teaspoon of non-diary creamer, flat, and two sugar cubes.

"Please."

"And what? I'm supposed to give you a performance spot?"

Flakes of instant coffee sprung to the surface of the mug like so much shipwrecked debris while the creamer became lumps of volcanic lava transformed into pumice by cool, salted waters.

Why did this young man unnerve him so that Bart had forgotten how to boil water?

Ben couldn't figure why this one should be so angry towards him. He had not sprayed his land or killed his prey. Ben turned his thoughts to the hairless ugly ones and their place to call home. He resisted the urge to bite this man. A growl was born in his heart, but with thoughts of Sally he swallowed. He spoke the words she had taught him. "No sir, I want to run the carousel."

"And where will that get you?" The reply, as rapid as a snake bite.

Ben didn't understand the question. He ran the question through again. "… where will that get you?" He still didn't understand. He knew that the carousel gallops in circles. He had watched it and had never seen it do anything but gallop in circles.

Like a dog chasing his tail, Ben saw the answer.

Ben left the tent with a blue apron and a funny looking metal thing that Bart had called a key. It felt unfamiliar and forbidding held in his teeth. He dropped it when he said "Hello" to the people who said "Hello" to him.

Bart ate his burnt food and lukewarm coffee and it was good. Maybe the kid wasn't that bad after all.

Lester and Lestim hugged Bart in turn. It had been so long since they had hugged him. They'd never hugged him as a grownup. They barely talked. Lester and Lestim were always in their own world. And their own world had moved farther and farther away. Bart didn't mind. He liked living alone and the daily chores of cleaning and feeding them had become habit. He missed the little giggles but, as grownup children, they had turned to hums. Droning hums they would use to communicate with one to another.

Tonight, they smelled Ben on Bart and felt scared. Felt they might lose this one who only gives. Lester and

Lestim didn't understand the money Bart made on them. They leaned against Bart, resting their heads on his shoulder, taking his arms to wrap around themselves. They swayed to their hums. Bart swayed with them. He hoped no one else was watching as he felt his eyes burn into the back of his head. He would have to start combing his hair a different way.

That night they watched Bart sleep. Lestim watched his head. Lester watched his feet. At 3:00 they traded sides. Neither saw his eyelids flutter or the rhododendron that filled his night. Bart slept soundly. He was with family.

When he woke, he remembered when he had last dreamed rhododendron. He drank from a mug of coffee that said, "World's Greatest Dad." A Mercedes roared by. A man sat with window open, waved his hand heartily. He winked his crescent shape brow. Bart smelled the cooking of bacon. That odor rested over morning dew on a thick plush lawn. Children's laughter came from inside the house. The laughter made him smile. He didn't know why. He woke. Lester and Lestim slept. Their eyelids fluttered. They dreamed.

POST-FRANKIE

After Frankie's head exploded, a bake sale was held. There were gingerbread men and women, brownies with and without nuts, and a lemon meringue pie that fell quickly. The monies needed to bury Frankie were raised. The coffin was simple and closed.

Bart sold his Oldsmobile to a car connoisseur who lacked the fine eye that could delineate between classic and crap. While counting his money, Bart tried to remember the day when his mode of transportation had become an antique. He took his place on the beaded seat cover behind the wheel of the converted school bus that was Frankie's Odditorium. Bart was to lead the caravan.

The Odditorium wasn't much of an attraction anymore. Frankie would present his peculiar program as his patriarchs had proudly performed in the past. That was his plan. He would show how it should be done, how it once was done, how it was no longer done, whenever he saw some son-of-a-bitchin' dirt-eating slacker of a lazy whore playing in his yard without pulling his weeds.

Frankie would pitch a crowd, round them in through the velvet ropes down the aisle of the bus, past the shrunken heads, wood from Noah's ark, heel bone from the first elephant assassinated in America, and a two-headed goat floating in a large mahogany tank. Frankie

171

would pull another quarter from the pockets of the shit eaters who couldn't guess which side of a coin was the tail. He never took in more than twenty dollars on a day, even on a Sunday. Now Frankie lay buried without a head. Once his mother kissed his little pink feet.

Prince Raphael's Odditorium had a different meaning to those who followed behind the strange, old bus. It was the old building not torn down, the old folk who pisses themself during family dinners yet remains an invited guest. It was the one box that is moved from home to home though never unpacked; a connection to a past that gave the followers certain rights to breathe and eat and copulate. Their right to a future was verified through history. Frankie was the guidepost; the bus—the beacon. Now it was Bart. No one argued when he took the wheel. Some smirked while others shook their heads. They knew their future was in capable hands, though they feared for their yesterdays.

Lester and Lestim strolled tentatively onto the bus. They stored their valise under the back-to-back seat Bart had bolted down for them. Staring out the window painted opaque in aqua and purple and orange. They imagined arches of gold and cars of red and blue and green. Lester scraped some paint from the window. Lestim felt four blue eyes stare at him as he waited his turn to scrape paint from the window. Kaufman bobbed in the tank. His eyes swam yes and no; never finding a moment's sleep. A blanket of dust covered his tank. Frankie would have crumbled up some newspaper and swiped the dust away. Bart did not. He was too close to the never-sleeping goat, whose endless staring screamed justice and cried mercy, though he had but one name.

An old man stood in the middle of the highway. He wore a thick wool coat with beaver collar. His derby hat seemed a bit too big as it slipped down, concealing all but the tip of his nose and full wet lips. He waved his silver-tipped cane in the air. Swerving to miss Raphael, the side of the road gave way. Though Bart turned the wheel right, the bus flipped left.

Kaufman's tank broke in two. The formaldehyde spilled through the broken glass and into the gravel of the deteriorated roadbed. The old man with the expensive clothing picked up the two-headed kid and placed it in a wooden pushcart. He left his diamond stick pin in exchange. Raphael wasn't an honest man, wasn't a fair man. He was a businessman.

They all rushed to note the fright and panic. It was as if it would be their turn next if they did not witness it. Lester and Lestim cried like babies once again. "Too bad" and "What a shame" were shared and exchanged with "It's a miracle no one was killed."

Bart recouped what the accident cost by pawning the diamond. His new minivan was easier to handle on the city streets and his keep still had the room they needed. He was glad to be done with all those strange, dead things. They weren't much of an attraction anymore and to Bart they held no real value.

When you die, stipulate that they bury you with two

bits in your pocket because, up in heaven, that is what Raphael is charging to view Nimiz, Ancient God of Mesopotamia. It's well worth the price in any lifetime.

THE MOST BEAUTIFUL WOMAN
IN THE WORLD

"I heard the most beautiful woman in the world is here," Bart said with his obligatory smirk as he made his way through the maze of lavender and gold.

She reached for her powder puff. Creating smoke before fire. "See for yourself."

Sam had her voice amplified in just so a method that Bart felt like he was being followed and preceded. It seemed as if he was crashing a merry-go-round. A breeze caused the curtains to flutter along with Bart's heart.

Bart remembered when Sam stole quarters and was caught. Now he has a show that could make Bart come undone. Kids today. He tried to think about what a good idea the spinning light was and how there was just the right amount of perfume in the air. How should Lester and Lestim smell? Betty, he remembers how she smelled and the girl she was, named Nancy. Betty, Bart had heard she was dead or married, and has no reason to doubt it. The mirror caught his eye.

"I was once only a woman who sat with a mirror and before that, a cute child, an attractive young woman. They had marked me wrong. Step a little closer, and you will see the most beautiful woman in the world."

Bart would swear the voice sounded familiar. Bart

would swear often, but would never swear to. Hardly ever at all; stick a needle in my eye.

"Why do you hold your breath?" The scented powder fashioned flowers from her words.

"I'm not holding my breath." How could she know when her prize was beauty and not wisdom?

The light from the mirror wouldn't let go. It wasn't that it grabbed tightly. It was more a passive hold that tightens when resisted.

"I heard you breathe. Now you stop. You breathe like your air is bought on layaway with a payday loan. Who do you owe? How much is it worth? How much then? How much now?"

Bart reached from the suckin city of Atlantis gasping for month to month minimum due.

"No! Don't hold your breath." Though he did. Often before, she continued. "Breath free. You bought it. You own it. You paid it off. Now, burn it up. Burn it down."

Bart formed the retort in his mind. The words danced and teased, and occasionally got real close. He was going to win this one but his tongue turned brittle and his mouth was dust. He said "Ghochff".

Her laughter was the cold shower on the hot day when the water stings and bites like so many happy bristles. Then the most beautiful woman in the world fell silent, as if serious. She asked a question. "What is the value of X?" Blue crepe paper streamers grazed over the white picket fences and red barns painted, two dimensional, on butcher's brown paper decorating the gymnasium walls. A timeless theme for a timeless time being that time. The boys and the girls danced and stood and slumped or shifted from one foot to another in a combination of the above.

Bart sees the old days all but forgotten. Deformed by lies and time. In his head he plays a Norman Rockwell video with a Frank Sinatra soundtrack to a rock n' roll beat.

Yeah, no date, *per se*, but there she was. She and Bobby, Bobby-boy Robby, Bobby Robert dancing in an oasis of Old Spice and Chanel numbers one through twenty-five. Under flat fluorescent light their skin glowed pink, not green. When he saw her dance, he knew the wet dog on the cold day who leans against the windowpane for some human warmth. Bart slipped another jigger of whiskey into the punch. When Diane stopped to catch her breath, with a smile and a laugh and with mercy and grace. Perspired and exhilarated, she reached for the drink that Bart had drawn with his own power. A thank you was spoken and there was a kiss, knee numbing, hair raising, lightning striking. As if the whole body was made from the fabric of the lips. "I'm blind!" shouted Bart. Everyone laughed and thought it a good joke. Robert took the arm of his sister and led her away. They half apologized to the world for their early departure, but they were leaving early in the morn for the Grandparents. But that we all knew. The dance was over. Bart removed his hands from his eyes. Slowly the world drifted back into focus.

Damn that Sam, where did he get a show like this?

Dancing with Diane, kissing Diane. The brief moment that was his fiction and his fact. The voice sounds so familiar.

He never thought he'd see Diane behind the gauze, through the flashing light, a reflection in a mirror. The powder settles on her breast.

Running from the tent he hears her say, "I'm no longer a pretty little girl, Bart Barker. I'm the most beautiful woman in the world."

"Diane."

Pity the poet and curse the knowing, whispered tales when their only license is to drive. Bless them for keeping love a mystery, hidden in a kiss in a dream.

She heard him speak, "Diane." It was the name of a stranger that made her twitch deep inside. The woman in the mirror saw the light in her eyes but nothing else. "Diane," a call again, and she looked deeper into the mirror and spun her supine fingers through her chestnut hair. She heard him cry, "Diane." The light grew hot and burnt her hand. The broken mirror added seven years to her account.

"Bart," she said without poetry. He ran from the tent.

Stands of fabric flowed through his fingers. He said, "Diane."

When Sam came to collect on the damages Bart had done to his curtains, he found him in bed and Lester and Lestim acting mother/fatherly, taking turns stirring soup, chicken, of course. They had learned to share. Bart had taught a lesson. Lester and Lestim had learned it.

Sam bragged about the money he was making while he complained it really wasn't his kind of work. Burn-out, you know. He gestured wildly with his left hand to show off the new pinky ring he was wearing as he told Bart his plans to get his real estate license, find a girl, change her name to Sally, marry, and have three children. Bart asked with a half-smile if Sam would have a seat, make himself comfortable. Sam declined, claimed to be busy, and left, saying he wished he could find someone appropriate to take over his pit show. He handed Bart the bill for reparations. "We'll talk," they both agreed.

PROLOGUE

Once upon a time, twins swam in the lake of their birth. Having yet to form a gender, they could be called female. It was dark and it was warm, and the moment of their conception had occurred and was forgotten. The soft tissue that was to become a skull taped together as the two selves who were intended to be siblings bounced with the rolling movement of maternal footsteps. The red walls that were eyelids faced one another. A smile never has appeared on the mouth without the prerequisite lips. Their thumbs, nestled in mittens that were the one, two, three, four, five fingers of each hand. They would be counted again, but for now there were one, two, three, four, five. The thumb so protected in its fetal fist. Later it would be key in proving apes need not live here. The toes would be counted too: one, two, three, four, five. The cord that provided the nourishment to what would be life was gripped in the hand not yet a hand. One took the cord and wrapped it around the other's neck: one, two. As the siblings bounced to the rolling of maternal footsteps, the cord became tighter and crimped: one. In a state of neither wake nor sleep, she died. One of two became one. Half became whole. Less was more than twice as much.

Mother stained. There was worry in the household

that disappeared under the doctor's assurance that all was normal. They had not lost the babe. The child was to be born a male. He was an only child. We'll call him Bart. It's a strong name.

BART

He is running. Running from a wall of water that chases him around the world; a never-ending sprint as the tide brings our one ocean on a circular tour of our flat, barren planet. A woman sits high atop a mountain. The only rise of land on the globe. She calls to the dreamer. "Climb up here to me. You'll be safe." As he stumbles up the mountain, he calls, "Diane." The ground crumbles beneath him. It is a mountain made of bones.

"You'll be safe with me."

Bart's fever broke.

He could see himself in her vanity mirror before it turned its back; his face, side by side with hers as she pulls the mohair brush through the strands of her hair.

The sawdust floor absorbs his tears. He cannot hear the chair scrape across the floor as she stands on her petite feet approaching him in her Chinese slippers. He feels her arms around him and dreams he is falling, falling, to his knees. She opens her kimono. When she is pressed against Bart, he begins to hear her sweat. Somewhere there is a kiss.

Bart is carried away in the singular ocean that leaves no beach behind.

A field mouse scurries past their heads, picks up a small butt of a Lucky, then returns to fortify its nest.

Did he kick the chair? Did he jump? Did he slowly bend his knees, yes followed by yes, with no space for no? There was no time to remember.

He left a note. Lester is the girl, Lestim is the boy. They like chicken.

On the back of the paper would be a list: butterfly wings, baby's breath, and one last dance. And he did dance among the ribbons of lavender and gold.

LESTER & LESTIM

"Pss't, girlie, you got a cigarette, girlie?"

Lester and Lestim heard the woman hiss though the fence to hidden faces behind closed shades. Neither took notice. They sat, each holding a mirror over their left shoulder. They looked into their sibling's eyes. They were blue and green and grey and black and brown and yellow and red.